'I'm the one at a disadvantage, if you were hoping I was Will.

'I'm James. The other Rowling. Will is my brother.'

'Brother? Oh,' Bella drawled as it hit her. 'You and Will are twins.'

'Guilty.' His eyes twinkled, sucking her under his spell for a moment.

'Then I'm doubly sorry.' With no small amount of regret, she reeled back her less-than-innocent interest. 'It's fine, really.'

It was not fine. It was so the opposite of fine, she couldn't even wrap her head around how not fine it was. Because she'd just realized this sensually intriguing man she'd accidentally tripped over was the brother of the man her father wanted her to marry.

If that didn't complicate her life a million times over, she didn't know what would.

Her hand was still gripped tightly in his and he didn't seem in any hurry to let her go. But he should. She pulled free and crossed her arms, wishing for a cover-up. Why did that glint in James's eye cause her to feel so exposed all at once?

The Princess and the Player

KAT CANTRELL

First published in Great Britain 2015
by Mills & Boon, an imprint of Harlequin (UK) Limited,
Large Print edition 2015
Eton House, 18-24 Paradise Road,
Richmond, Surrey, TW9 1SR

Special thanks and acknowledgement are given to Kat Cantrell for her contribution to the *Dynasties: The Montoros* miniseries.

ISBN: 978-0-263-26043-4

Harlequin (UK) Limited's policy is to use papers that are natural, renewable and recyclable products and made from wood grown in sustainable forests. The logging and manufacturing processes conform to the legal environmental regulations of the country of origin.

Printed and bound in Great Britain
by CPI Antony Rowe, Chippenham, Wiltshire

KAT CANTRELL

read her first Mills & Boon® novel in third grade and has been scribbling in notebooks since she learned to spell. What else would she write but romance? She majored in literature, officially with the intent to teach, but somehow ended up buried in middle management in corporate America, until she became a stay-at-home mom and full-time writer.

Kat, her husband and their two boys live in north Texas. When she's not writing about characters on the journey to happily-ever-after, she can be found at a soccer game, watching the TV show *Friends* or listening to '80s music.

Kat was the 2011 Mills & Boon® So You Think You Can Write winner and a 2012 RWA Golden Heart Award finalist for best unpublished series contemporary manuscript.

One

Auwck. Auwck.

Bella Montoro's eyelids flew open at the raucous and unwelcome alarm clock. One of the pair of feral blue-and-gold macaws who lived in the tree outside the window of her Coral Gables mansion had chosen today, of all days, to wake her early.

Miami was full of wild macaws and normally, she loved them. Today, not so much.

Groaning, she smooshed a pillow over her head but the pressure didn't ease her champagne head-ache and the barrier didn't muffle the happy squawks of her feathered friend. Fine. It was time to drag herself out of bed anyway.

She sat up. A glance through the bay window confirmed which bird it was.

"Good morning, Buttercup," she muttered sarcastically, but with the window closed, the macaw couldn't hear her.

She didn't dare open the window for fear she'd frighten her away. Both Buttercup and her mate, Wesley, were as wild as the day was long, and Bella enjoyed it when they deigned to hang out with her. She watched them groom themselves for as long as she dared since she wouldn't get to see them for a while once she left Miami for the small country of Alma—today's destination.

Bella had always known she was descended from royalty, but a dictator had been ruling her ancestor's country for ages. She'd never expected the political climate to shift. Or for the Montoros to reclaim the throne. But it had happened and though her father was first in line to become king, his divorce rendered him ineligible for the crown due to Alma's strict laws. Then her oldest brother, Rafe, had abdicated his place so he could focus on the new baby he and his fiancée, Emily, were expecting.

Her other brother, Gabriel, had stepped up, adopting his new role with an ease Bella admired. And while she liked the tiny island country of Alma well enough to go back for her brother's coronation as the new king, the promise of bigger and better parties didn't fully make up for having to leave behind the things she loved in Miami.

She was also leaving behind her great-aunt Isabella, who might draw her last breath any day now. Rafe would check in on her of course, and Bella could call. But still. It wasn't the same as having daily access to the woman who always had a kind word and gentle piece of advice, no matter what the occasion. Bella had been named for her father's aunt, and they shared a kinship that transcended age.

Her father owed her for agreeing to this move to Alma. Big time.

Bella watched Buttercup groom her feathers for a moment, and then turned away from the beautiful view of the grounds. She might not see this house again either, and she'd taken for granted how much she loved living here. Now that the day of her departure had arrived, everything had gotten real, really fast. She'd been an American her whole life and while she'd always enjoyed the privileges of being a Montoro, becoming a member of Alma's royal family carried heavy responsibilities with few tangible rewards.

Not that anyone had asked her opinion.

With far too much racket for Bella's taste, her maid, Celia, bustled into the bedroom and frowned at the crumpled, glittery dress on the floor as she stepped over it. "They have plenty more hangers at the store if you've run out, Miss Bella."

Bella grinned at the woman who'd been her friend, confidant and occasional strong shoulder for years, blessing her for sticking to their tried-and-true teasing instead of becoming maudlin over the irreversible changes that had ripped through the Montoro family recently.

"Got hangers," Bella informed her around an involuntary yawn. "Just not the will to use one at three a.m."

Celia sniffed as if displeased, but an indulgent smile tugged at her mouth nonetheless. "Seems like a gal about to get on a plane in a few hours might come home at a decent hour."

"Oh, but it was my last night in Miami!" Bella protested without any real heat and stretched with a moan. "I had lots of people to see. Lots of parties to attend."

"Hmpf. Lots of money to talk your friends out of, you mean."

Celia was one of the few people who recognized that Bella's involvement in wildlife conservation wasn't just a rich girl's cute hobby. It was Bella's passion and she used her connections. Shamelessly. And it wasn't an accident that she'd been named the top fund-raiser in Florida by two different conservation groups.

"You say that like it's a bad thing." Bella shook her head as Celia selected an outfit from the overflowing closet and held it out with a raised eyebrow. "Not that one. The blue pantsuit for the plane. With the cropped jacket."

Like a well-rehearsed ballet, Bella and Celia danced around each other as they navigated a bedroom that closely resembled a post-hurricane department store. Everyone joked that you could always tell when Bella had whirled through a scene because nothing was in one piece afterward. It was a reference to Bella's birth during the harrowing hours of Hurricane Andrew, before FEMA had started cracking down on evacuations.

Both mother and baby had emerged from the storm without incident, but Bella held the private belief that the experience had branded her soul with hurricane-like qualities she couldn't shake. Not the least of which was a particular talent for causing chaos.

Celia began packing Bella's suitcases while her mistress dressed and they laughed over Bella's account of the previous night's parties, as they'd done many a morning over the years. But this would be the last time for a long time. Maybe forever, depending on what happened in Alma.

Bella kept up the light banter, but she was pretty sure the shadows in Celia's eyes were reflected in her own. As the hour grew near for Bella to leave for the sun-drenched islands of Alma, she couldn't stand it any longer. "I wish you could go with me to Alma!"

And then to her mortification, Bella burst into tears.

Celia folded Bella into her arms and they clung to each other. When Adela, Bella's mom, had finally ditched her cold, unsatisfying marriage the day after Bella's eighteenth birthday, Celia had been the one who stuck around to make sure Bella didn't

get into too much trouble. Best of both worlds—
she had someone who cared, but who also couldn't
tell her what to do. Bella did not like being told
what to do.

"There, now. Your brother will look out for you
and besides, you'll be having so much fun as the
new princess, you won't even notice I'm not there."

"That's not true," Bella sniffed and hugged
Celia tighter. "Gabriel will be busy with king stuff
and spend all his free time with Serafia now that
they're getting married. What if I'm banished to
some out of the way place—*alone*?"

She wouldn't put it past her father to lock her up
in the palace dungeon or do something else equally
archaic since he seemed bent on rediscovering his
old-fashioned side. That last photo of her to hit the
tabloids? Totally not her fault. How was she supposed to know the paparazzi had hidden in the
foliage surrounding Nicole's pool? Everyone else
had shed their swimsuits, too, but Bella was the
only one they'd targeted, of course.

Rafael Montoro the Third was not amused. Apparently it was problematic that her father's business associates and soon-to-be-king Gabriel's

future subjects in Alma could easily access naked photos of Bella.

No one seemed to remember that she was the victim in that scandal.

Celia snorted. "With Gabriel about to take the throne, your father will want the whole family in the public eye, gaining support for your brother. You're the only princess Alma's got, sweetie. They'll love you and so will your fiancé. Your father can't lock you away *and* expect you to marry the man he's picked out."

"Yeah, I've been trying not to think about that." Her head started pounding again and that fourth glass of champagne last night started to feel like a bad idea. But her friends had been determined to send her off in style to her new life as the sister of the king of Alma, so how could she refuse?

Besides, anything that helped her forget the arranged marriage her father was trying to force down her throat was a plus in her book. Fine time for her father to remember he had a daughter—when it was important for the Montoro family to strengthen ties with Alma through marriage. How come Gabriel and Rafe didn't have to marry someone advantageous? Her brothers had chosen their own brides. It wasn't fair. But her father had made it clear she was to get on a plane and meet this man Will Rowling, who was the son of one of Alma's most powerful businessmen.

Maybe she should be thankful no one had thought to match her with Will's father. Seemed as if that might be more advantageous than marrying the son. She shuddered. *No* marriage sounded like fun, no matter who the guy was.

If Alma turned out to be horrible, she'd just come home. Rafe and Emily were going to make her an aunt soon, and she'd love to hang out in Key West with the baby. Nobody dictated Bella's life but her.

"Mr. Rafael isn't completely unreasonable. After all, he did agree to let you meet Will and see how things go. Just remember why you're doing this," Celia advised.

Bella's guilty conscience reared its ugly head and she eased out of Celia's embrace before the older woman sensed it. "It's my royal obligation to help Gabriel ascend to the throne," she mimicked in her father's deep voice. "The whole family needs to be in Alma to prepare for the coronation."

But that wasn't really why she'd agreed to go. Miami had grown too small to hold both Bella and

Drew Honeycutt. Honestly, when you told a guy that you just wanted to have fun and not take a relationship seriously, he was supposed to breathe a sigh of relief.

He was not supposed to fall to one knee and propose after two months of casual dating. And then plaster his second proposal on twenty billboards around the city, along with Bella's picture and a cartoon heart around her face. The third proposal spread across the sky in the form of a "Will you marry me, Bella Montoro?" banner behind a small plane, which flew up and down South Beach for six hours while Bella was at a private cookout on the penthouse terrace of Ramone, the new guy she'd been seeing. A fan of drama Ramone was not. Thanks to Drew, he'd bowed out.

And Bella had really liked Ramone, dang it; the more he drank, the more money he handed over for her wildlife charities.

Drew followed her around, popping up at parties and museum openings like a bad penny, espousing his love for Bella with horrific poetry and calf eyes galore. It would be great if she could tell him off, but Honeycutt Logistics did a lot of business with Montoro Enterprises and she couldn't afford to irritate her father further. Plus, she was 97 percent sure Drew was harmless and worse, he seemed genuinely baffled and brokenhearted over her continual rejection of his proposals.

Each Drew sighting was another kick to the stomach. Another reminder that she was the hurricane baby, destined to whirl through people's lives and leave havoc in her wake. If only she could find a way to *not* break everything into little pieces—even though it was always an accident—she'd feel a lot better. She hated hurting people.

It was probably not a bad plan to disappear from the Miami scene for a while.

Celia managed to get Bella into the car on time and with all her luggage. The gates parted and Bella waved goodbye to Buttercup, Wesley and the house she'd grown up in as the driver picked up speed and they exited the grounds. Sun sparkled across Biscayne Bay and her spirits rose with each mile marker along the highway to the private airstrip where the Montoro Enterprises jet waited to fly her to Alma.

This was an adventure no matter what and she was going to enjoy every second of the sun, sand

and royal parties ahead. By the time she'd boarded the plane, buckled her seatbelt and accepted a mimosa from Jan—the same flight attendant who'd given her crayons and coloring books once upon a time—Bella's mood had turned downright cheerful. Cheerful enough to sneak a glance at the picture of Will Rowling her father had sent her.

He was classically handsome, with nice hair and a pleasant smile. The serious glint in his eye might be a trick of the light. Serious she could do without and besides, this was the guy her *father* had picked. Chances were Will and Bella would get on like oil and water.

But she'd reserve judgment until she met him because first and foremost, Alma was about starting fresh and Will deserved a chance to prove they were meant for each other. If he came out strong with a fun-loving nature and swept her off her feet, she'd be okay with a fabulous love affair and passion to spare.

Though she couldn't deny that one of the big question marks was what kind of guy would agree to an arranged marriage in the twenty-first century. There was probably something really wrong with Will Rowling if he couldn't meet women on his own. She probably had a better chance of her plane flying into an alternate universe than finding her soul mate in Will Rowling.

For the fourth time, someone kicked sand in James Rowling's face and for the fourth time, he ignored it. If he let loose with a string of curses—the way he wanted to—he'd only alert someone to his presence here, and James was trying to be invisible.

Or at least as invisible as one of Alma's most notorious failures could be. Maybe in fifty years he could fade into the woodwork, but every single citizen of Alma—and probably most of the free world—had watched him miss that goal in the World Cup. Anonymity was scarce.

So far, no one had recognized him with Oakleys covering his eyes and a backward ball cap over his hair. The longer he kept it that way, the better. The last thing he wanted was a bunch of questions about why Real Madrid had dropped his contract. It wasn't hard to look that one up…along with pictures of James leaving a bar in Rio with a prostitute…not that she'd mentioned money to *him*. Or worse, questions about whether he planned to stick around his adopted homeland and play for Alma's reserve football team—*soccer* team if the questioner was American.

No comment.

A reserve team was for beginners. He would get a new professional league contract, period. If not around here, then maybe back in England, where he'd been born. There was no other alternative. Football was his life.

Peeling his shirt away from his sticky chest, he leaned back into his short-legged beach chair, stuck his legs straight out and closed his eyes, somehow sure the elusive measure of peace he sought would be within reach this time. He almost snorted. When had he turned into an optimist?

There was no peace to be had and if there was, it sure as hell wouldn't be found in Alma, the capital of boring. Not to mention his father's presence permeated the entire island, as if Patrick Rowling's soul lived in the bedrock, sending out vibrations of disapproval on a regularly scheduled basis.

That's why James was at the beach at Playa Del Onda, soaking up the sun instead of doing whatever it was his father thought he should be doing, which would never happen because James lacked the capacity to do what his father said. It was like a mutated gene: his father spoke and James's brain refused to obey. He automatically did the opposite.

"*Ooof!*" Air whooshed from his lungs as something heavy landed square on his chest.

Then his beach chair flipped, tossing him into the sand on top of something. It squealed.

Some*one*. When his vision cleared, the tangle of supple-bodied woman and blond hair underneath him captured his complete attention.

He gazed down into the bluest set of eyes he'd seen in a while. Something shifted inside as the woman blinked back, her beautiful heart-shaped face reflecting not an iota of remorse over their risqué position. Her body had somehow slid into the grooves of his effortlessly and the slightest incline of his head would fuse his lips to hers.

She'd fully gobsmacked him.

Their breath intermingled. She seemed in no hurry to unstick her skin from his and in about two and a half seconds, his own body would start getting into the moment in a huge and inappropriate way.

Sexy strangers signaled big-time problems and he had enough of those.

Reluctantly, he rolled off her and helped her sit up. "Sorry about that. You okay?"

"Totally." Her husky voice skittered across his skin and he was hooked on the sound of it instantly. American. His favorite. "My fault. I was focused on this thing instead of where I was going."

She kicked at a Frisbee he hadn't noticed lying in the sand two feet away. But who'd pay attention to a piece of plastic when a fit blonde in a tiny bikini landed in your lap? Not him.

"I like a girl who goes for the memorable introduction."

It was certainly a new one. And he'd experienced his share of inventive ploys for getting his attention. Knickers with cell phone numbers scrawled in marker across the crotch, which he discovered had been shoved into his pocket. Room keys slipped into drinks sent over by a knot of football groupies at a corner table. Once, he'd gone back to his hotel room after a press junket to find two naked women spread out across his bed. How they'd gotten in, he still didn't know.

The logistics question had sort of slipped his mind after ten minutes in their company.

"Oh, I wasn't angling for an introduction." She

actually blushed a bit, which was oddly endearing. "I really didn't see you there. You kind of blend into the sand."

"Is that a crack about my British complexion?" he teased. "You're pretty pale yourself, darling."

She laughed and rearranged her hair, pulling it behind her back so it didn't conceal her cleavage. A move he thoroughly appreciated. This gorgeous klutz might be the best thing that had happened to him all week. Longer than that. The best thing since arriving in Alma for sure.

Maybe it wasn't so bad to be stuck here cooling his heels until a football club whose jersey he could stomach wearing knocked on his door.

"No, not at all. I wouldn't be so rude as to point out your flaws on our first meeting." She leaned forward, her vibe full of come-hither as she teased him back.

Intrigued, he angled his head toward her. "But on our second date, all bets are off?"

Glancing down coquettishly, she let loose a small smile. "I'm more of a third-date kind of girl."

His gut contracted as the full force of that promise hit him crossways. She was a unique breed of woman, the most fascinating one he'd met thus far on this stupid rock he was being forced to call home for the time being. The memory of her hot flesh against his was still fresh—it was enough to drive him mad. And he suspected she knew exactly what she was doing to him.

"I have a feeling you'd be worth the wait."

She picked that moment to stand and for some reason, the new angle cast her in a different light. It tickled his mind and he recognized her all at once. Pictures of the new princess had graced every news channel for the past couple of weeks, but she'd been clothed. Regardless, he should have recognized her sooner and maybe not disgraced himself by flirting with a woman who probably really had no clue she'd stumbled over a former football player for Real Madrid.

A princess—especially one as fit as Bella Montoro—wasn't running around the beach at Playa Del Onda looking to meet guys, whether they were semifamous or not. Which was a dirty shame.

He shoved his hat back onto his head and repositioned his sunglasses, both of which had flown off during the sand tango.

Ms. Montoro... Princess Bella... Your Royal Highness... What did you even call her when her brother hadn't been crowned yet? Whatever the form of address, she was way out of his league.

But that didn't mean she thought so. She hadn't bothered to hide the frank attraction in her gaze when she'd been in his arms earlier. If there was anything he knew, it was women, and she might be royalty but that didn't necessarily make her off-limits.

He quickly scrambled to his feet in case there was some protocol for standing when princesses stood...even if she was wearing a postage stamp–sized white bikini that somehow covered everything while leaving nothing to the imagination.

No point in beating around the bush. "Am I permitted to call you Bella or is there some other title you'd prefer?"

"What, like *Princess*?" She wrinkled her nose. "I'm not really used to all that yet. And besides, I think we're a little past that stage, don't you?"

The feel of her soft curves flush against his body flooded his mind and his board shorts probably wouldn't conceal his excitement much longer if he didn't cool his jets. "Yeah. Formality isn't my specialty anyway. Bella it is."

Strangely, calling her Bella ratcheted up the intimacy quotient by a thousand. He liked it. And he wanted to say it a bunch more times while she lay stretched out under him again. Without the bikini.

She smiled and glanced down, as if the heat roiling between them was affecting her, too, and she didn't know quite what to do with it. "This is all so awkward. I wasn't sure you knew who I was."

Shrugging, he stuck his hands behind his back because he had no clue what to do with them. It was the first time he'd been unsure around a woman since the age of fourteen. "I recognized you from your pictures."

She nodded and waved off her friend who'd most likely come to investigate the disappearance of her Frisbee partner. "Me, too. I wasn't expecting to run into you on the beach or I would have dressed for the occasion."

Ah, so she *did* know who he was—and dare he hope there was a hint of approval there? She'd gotten rid of the friend, a clear sign she planned to stick around for a while at least. Maybe he wasn't so far out of her league after all. "I'm a fan of your wardrobe choice."

Laughing, she glanced down. "I guess it is appropriate for the beach, isn't it? It's just not how

I thought meeting you would go. The picture my father sent painted you as someone very serious."

"Um…you don't say?" He'd just completely lost the thread of the conversation. Why would her father be sending her pictures, unless… Of course. Had to make sure the precious princess didn't taint herself with the common riffraff. *Stay away from that Rowling boy. He's a boatload of trouble.*

His temper kicked up, but he smoothed it over with a wink and a wicked smile. "I'm every bit as bad as your father warned you. Probably worse. If your goal is to seriously irritate him, I'm on board with that."

He had no problem being her Rebel Against Daddy go-to guy, though he'd probably encourage her to be *really* bad and enjoy it far too much. Instantly, a few choice scenarios that would get them both into a lot of trouble filled his mind.

Her eyes widened. "He, uh, didn't warn me about you… Actually, I'm pretty sure he'd be happy if we went out. Isn't that the whole point of this? So we can see if we're suited?"

This conversation was going in circles. Her father wanted them to date? "He's a football fan, then?"

She shook her head, confusion clouding her gaze. "I don't think so. Does that matter to you, Will?"

"Will?" He groaned. This was so much worse than he'd anticipated. "You think I'm Will?"

More importantly, her father had sent her a picture of Will for some yet-to-be-determined reason, but it wasn't so she could flirt with Will's twin brother on the beach. And this little case of mistaken identity was about to come to an abrupt halt.

Two

Bella laced her fingers together as she got the impression all at once that she wasn't talking to the man she thought she was. "Aren't you Will Rowling?"

He had to be. She'd studied his picture enough on the plane and then again last night while she tried to go to sleep but couldn't, because she'd been wondering what in the world her father was thinking with this arranged marriage nonsense. And then she'd come to the beach with the daughter of one of the servants who was close to her age, only to trip over said man her father had selected.

Except he was staring at her strangely and the

niggle of doubt wormed its way to the surface again. How could she have made such a mistake?

"Not Will. Not even close," he confirmed.

He grinned, and she let herself revel in his gorgeous aqua-colored eyes for a moment because she didn't have to fight an attraction to him if he wasn't the man her father picked out for her.

The sun shone a little brighter and the sea sparkled a bit bluer. Digging her toes into the warm sand that suddenly felt heavenly against her bare feet, she breathed a sigh of relief and grinned back.

This was turning out better than she'd hoped. Geez, she'd been one heartbeat away from believing in love at first sight and trying for all she was worth to shut it down. Because she'd thought he was Will Rowling. Imagine *that*. Her father would be insufferable about it and demand they get married right away if she'd become smitten so fast. It would have been a disaster.

But if this extremely sexy man wasn't Will— *perfect*. She slid her gaze down his well-cut body, which a T-shirt and long shorts couldn't hide. Of course she'd felt every single one of his valleys and hard peaks. Intimately.

No. This was *not* perfect. She was supposed to

be meeting Will and seeing if they got along, not flirting with some look-alike stranger who made her itch to accept the wicked invitation in his gaze, which promised if he got her naked, he'd rock her world.

With no small amount of regret, she reeled back her less-than-innocent interest.

"Well, sorry about that, then," she said and held out her hand. Might as well start over since this whole thing had blown up in her face. "Bella Montoro. I guess you already knew that, but I'm at a disadvantage."

His rich laugh hit her a moment before he clasped her hand in his and the combination heated her more than the bright sun or her embarrassment. "I'm the one at a disadvantage, if you were hoping I was Will. I'm James. The other Rowling. Will is my brother."

"Brother? Oh," she drawled as it hit her. "You and Will are twins."

"Guilty." His eyes twinkled, sucking her under his spell for a moment.

"Then I'm doubly sorry." Mortified, she racked her brain, but if her father had told her Will had a twin brother, she surely would have remembered that. "I've made a complete mess out of this, haven't I?"

"Not at all. People confuse us all the time. It's fine, really."

It was not fine. It was so the opposite of fine, she couldn't even wrap her head around how *not fine* it was. Because she'd just realized this sensually intriguing man she'd accidentally tripped over was the *brother* of the intended target of her father's archaic arranged marriage plan.

If that didn't complicate her life a million times over, she didn't know what would.

Her hand was still gripped tight in his and he didn't seem in any hurry to let her go. But he should. She pulled free and crossed her arms, wishing for a cover-up. Why did that glint in James's eye cause her to feel so exposed all at once?

"I'm curious," James said casually as if the vibe between them had just cooled, which it most definitely had not. "Why did your father send you a picture of Will?"

"Oh, so I would know what he looks like." Actually, she'd demanded he do so. There was no way she was getting on a plane to meet someone blind.

"I'm sensing there's more to the story." His raised eyebrows encouraged her to elaborate.

"Wouldn't you wonder about the appearance of a person your father wanted you to marry? I sure did."

Surprise flew across James's face. "Your father wants you to marry Will? Does Will know about this?"

"Of course he does. Your father was the instigator, actually. You didn't know our fathers cooked up this idea of an arranged marriage?"

His laugh was far more derisive this time. "The elder Rowling doesn't share much of what goes on his head. But somehow it doesn't shock me to discover dear old Dad wants his son married to a member of the royal family. Did you agree?"

"No! Well, not yet anyway. I only agreed to meet Will and see what happened. I'm not really in the market for a steady relationship, let alone one as permanent as marriage."

Groaning, she bit her lip. Too late to take that back, though it had been the God-honest truth. Regardless, spilling her guts to the brother of her potential fiancé wasn't the best plan. James would probably run off and tell Will his future bride had felt up his brother on the beach—totally not her fault!—flirted with him—maybe partially her fault—and then declared marriage to be worse than the plague.

Instead of falling to his knees in shock, James winked and dang, even that was sexy.

"Woman after my own heart. If you don't want to get married, why even agree to meet Will?"

Why was she still standing here talking to the wrong brother? She should go. There was nothing for her here. But she couldn't make herself walk away from the spark still kicking between them.

"It's complicated," she hedged.

She sighed and glanced over her shoulder, but there was no one in earshot. She didn't want to draw the attention of a camera lens, but surely it couldn't hurt to spend a few minutes chatting with the man who might become her brother-in-law… so she could keep reminding herself that's who he was to her. If nothing else, she could set the record straight in case he intended to repeat this conversation verbatim to his brother.

"I'm the king of uncomplicating things," James said with another laugh that curled her toes deeper into the sand. "Try me."

It wasn't as if anyone was expecting her back at the gargantuan house perched on the cliff behind them. Gabriel was never home and her father... Well, she wasn't dying to run into him again.

She shrugged. "We're all new at this royalty thing. I don't want to be the one to mess it up. What if I don't try with Will and it has horrible repercussions for my brother Gabriel? I can't be responsible for that."

"But if you meet Will and you don't like him, how is that different than not meeting him in the first place? Either way, you don't end up with him and the repercussions will be the same."

How come she'd never thought of that? "That's a good point."

"Told you. I can uncomplicate anything. It's a skill." James's smile widened as he swept her with an impossible to misinterpret look. "I just figure out what I want to do and justify it. Like...if I wanted to kiss you, I'd find a way."

As his gaze rested on her lips, heat flooded her cheeks. And other places. She could practically feel the weight of his kiss against her mouth and he hadn't even moved. A pang of lust zinged through her abdomen and she nearly gasped at the strength of it. What was it about him that lit her up so fiercely?

"You shouldn't be talking about kissing." She inwardly cursed. That should have come out much more sternly, instead of breathy with anticipation. "Flirting as a whole is completely off-limits."

A hint of challenge crept into his expression and then he leaned in, stopping just short of touching her earlobe with his mouth. "Says who?"

"Me," she murmured as the scent of male and heat coiled up low in her belly, nearly making her weep with want. "I'm weak and liable to give in. You have to be the strong one and stop presenting me with so much temptation."

He laughed softly. "I'm afraid you're in a lot of trouble, then."

"Why?"

"Because I have absolutely no reservations about giving in to temptation."

The wicked smile spreading across his face sealed it—she *was* in a lot of trouble. She was supposed to marry his brother. And the last thing she needed was to set herself up for a repeat of the Drew Debacle, where she accidentally broke

James's heart because she ended up with Will. Better all around to stay away from James.

Why did the wrong Rowling have to be so alluring and so delicious?

Maybe she could find Will similarly attractive if she just gave him a chance.

"I'll keep that in mind." All right, then. She was going to have to be the one to step away. Noted.

So step away. Right now.

Through a supreme act of will, she somehow did. James's gorgeous aqua eyes tracked her movement as she put one foot, then two between them. He nodded once, apparently in understanding but definitely not in agreement.

"See you around, Princess."

He stood there, one hip cocked in a casual stance that screamed Bad Boy, and she half waved before she turned and fled.

As she climbed the stairs to the house, she resisted looking over her shoulder to see if she could pick out James's yellow T-shirt amidst the other sun worshippers lounging on the white sand. He wasn't for her and there was no getting around the fact that she wished otherwise.

James Rowling was forbidden. And that might be his most attractive quality.

Bella entered the Playa Del Onda house through the kitchen, and snagged a glass-bottled cola from the refrigerator and a piece of crusty bread from the pantry. Both the colas and the bread tasted different in Europe but she didn't mind. All part of the adventure.

Thoughts still on the sexy man she'd abandoned on the beach, Bella munched on the bread as she climbed the stairs to her bedroom. She almost made it before a dark shadow alerted her to the fact that her least favorite person in the house had found her.

"Isabella." Her father's sharp voice stopped her dead, four steps from the landing on the second floor.

"Yeah, Dad?" She didn't turn around. If you didn't stare him in the eye, he couldn't turn you to stone, right?

"Is that how you dress to go out?"

"Only when I go to the beach," she retorted. "Is there something new you'd like to discuss or shall we rehash the same subject from last night? You didn't like that outfit either, if I recall."

Ever since Adela, Bella's mother, had left, this is how it went. Her father only spoke to her when he wanted to tell her how to run her life. And she pretended to listen. Occasionally, when it suited her, she went along, but only if she got something out of it.

"We'll rehash it as many times as it takes to get it through your scattered brain. Gabriel is going to be *king.*" Rafael stressed the word as if she might be confused about what was happening around her. "The least you can do is help smooth his ascension with a little common sense about how you dress. The Montoros have no credibility yet, especially not with that stunt your brother pulled."

"Rafe fell in love," she shot back and bit her tongue.

Old news. Her father cared nothing for love, only propriety. And horror of all horrors—his eldest son had gotten a bartender pregnant and then abdicated the throne so he could focus on his new family. In Daddy's mind, it fell squarely into the category of impropriety. Unforgivable.

It was a reminder that her father also cared little for his daughter's happiness either. Only royal protocol.

"Rafe is a disappointment. I'll not have another child of mine follow his example." He cleared his throat. "Face me when we're speaking, please."

She complied, but only because the front view of her bikini was likely to give him apoplexy and she kind of wanted to see it.

He pursed his lips but, to her father's credit, that was his only reaction. "When have you arranged to meet Will Rowling?"

Ah, of course. Complaining about her bikini was a smoke screen—this was actually an ambush about her arranged marriage. With the scent of forbidden fruit lingering in her senses coupled with her father's bad attitude, she'd developed a sudden fierce desire to spend time with someone who had clearly never met a good time he didn't like.

And his name wasn't Will. "I haven't yet."

"What are you waiting for, an invitation? This is your match to make, Isabella. I'm giving you some latitude in the timing but I expect results. Soon." The severe lines around his mouth softened. "This alliance is very important. To the entire Montoro family and to the royal legacy of Alma. I'm not asking this for myself, but for Gabriel. Remember that."

She sighed. "I know. That's why I'm here. I do want to be a credit to the royal family."

Hurricane Bella couldn't whirl through Alma and disrupt the entire country. She knew that. Somehow, she had to be better than she'd been in Miami. The thought of Miami reminded her of Buttercup and Wesley, her feathered friends she'd left behind. Some said the wild macaws that nested in southern Florida were people's pets set free during Hurricane Andrew. She'd always felt an affinity with the birds because they'd all survived the storm. Buttercup and Wesley could continue to be her source of strength even from afar.

"Good. Then arrange to meet Will Rowling and do it soon. Patrick Rowling is one of the most influential men in Alma and the Montoros need his support. We cannot afford another misstep at this point."

It wasn't anything she hadn't heard before, but on the heels of meeting James, the warning weighed heavily on her shoulders. Gabriel hadn't wanted to be thrust suddenly into a starring role in the restoration of the monarchy to Alma's political land-scape. But he'd stepped up nonetheless. She could do the same.

But why did it matter which Rowling she married anyway? Surely one was as good as the other. Perhaps she could turn this to her advantage by seeing where things went with James.

"I'll do my best not to mess this up," Bella promised.

If it didn't matter which Rowling she picked, that meant she didn't need to call Will anytime soon. The reprieve let her breathe a little easier.

Her father raised his eyebrows. "That would be a refreshing change. On that note, don't assume that you left all the tabloids behind in Miami. The paparazzi know no national boundaries. Stay out of scandalous situations, don't drink too much and for God's sake, keep your clothes on."

She saluted saucily to cover the sharp spike of hurt that she never could seem to stop no matter how many times she told herself this was just how he was. "Yes, Father."

Escaping to her room, Bella took a long shower but it didn't ease the ache from the showdown with Rafael.

Why did she still care that her father never hugged her or told her he was proud of her? Not for the first time, she wondered if the frosty temperature in her father's demeanor had caused her mother to leave. If so, Bella hardly blamed her. She hoped Adela had found happiness.

Happiness should be the most important factor in whom you married. The thought solidified Bella's resolve. If her father wanted a match between the Montoros and the Rowlings, great. Bella would comply—as long as the Rowling was James.

She'd rather see where that led than try to force a match with the right brother.

Why shouldn't she be allowed to be as happy as Rafe and Gabriel?

The loud, scornful whispering at the next table over started to annoy James about two bites into his paella. Couldn't a bloke get something to eat without someone publicly crucifying him? This time, the subject of choice was his lack of a decision on whether to take a spot on Alma's reserve team.

The two middle-aged men were in complete agreement: James should be happy to have *any* position, even though Alma wasn't a UEFA team. He should take his lumps and serve his penance, and then it would be acceptable to play for a premiere club again, once he'd redeemed himself. Or so the men opined, and not very quietly.

The paella turned to sawdust in his mouth. He was glad someone knew what he needed to do next in his stalled career.

Playing for Alma was a fine choice. For a beginner. But James had been playing football since he was seven, the same year his father had uprooted his two sons from their Guildford home and moved them to the tiny, nowhere island of Alma. Football had filled a void in his life after the death of his mother. James loved the game. Being dropped from Real Madrid had stung, worse than he'd let on to anyone.

Of course, whom would he tell? He and Will rarely talked about anything of note, usually by James's choice. Will was the perfect son who never messed up, while James spent as much effort as he possibly could on irritating his father. James and Will might be twins but the similarities ended there—and Will was a Manchester United fan from way back, so they couldn't even talk football without almost coming to blows.

And Will had first dibs on the woman James hadn't been able to forget. All without lifting a finger. Life just reeked sometimes.

Unable to eat even one more bite of the dish he'd found so tasty just minutes ago, James threw a few bills on the table and stalked out of the restaurant into the bright afternoon sun on the boardwalk at Playa Del Onda.

So much for hanging out at the beach where fewer people might recognize him. He might as well go back to Del Sol and let his father tell him again how much of a disappointment he was. Or he could swallow his bitterness and get started on finding another football club since none had come looking for him.

A flash of blond hair ahead of him caught his eye. Since Bella had been on his mind in one way or another since he'd met her the day before, it was no wonder he was imagining her around every corner.

He shouldn't, though. She'd been reserved for the "right" Rowling, the one who could do no wrong. James's black sheep status hadn't improved much. Frankly, she deserved a shot at the successful brother, though he had no clue if Will was even on board with the match their father had apparently orchestrated. When Bella mentioned it yesterday, that was the first he'd heard of it. Which didn't mean it wasn't legit.

The woman in front of him glanced into a shop window and her profile confirmed it. It *was* Bella.

Something expanded in his chest and he forgot why he wasn't supposed to think about her. Unable to help himself all of a sudden, James picked up his pace until he drew up alongside her. "Fancy meeting you here."

Tilting her head down, she looked at him over the top of her sunglasses and murmured something reassuring to the burly security detail trailing her. They backed off immediately.

"James Rowling, I presume?" she said to him.

He laughed. "The one and only. Getting in some shopping?"

"Nope. Waiting around for you to stroll by. It's about time. I was starting to think you'd ordered everything on El Gatito's menu." She nodded in the direction of the restaurant he'd just exited and leaned in to murmur, "I hope you skipped the cat."

She'd been waiting for him? The notion tripped him up even more than her wholly American, wholly sexy perfume, for some odd reason.

"I, uh, did. Skip the cat," he clarified as he caught her joke in reference to the restaurant's name. "They were fresh out."

Her smile set off a round of sparks he'd rather not have over his brother's intended match.

"Maybe next time."

"Maybe next time you'll just come inside and eat with me instead of skulking around outside like a stalker," he suggested and curled his lip. What was he *doing*—asking her out? Bad idea.

One of her eyebrows quirked up above the frame of her sunglasses. "I can say with absolute authority that me noticing you heading into a restaurant and accidentally-on-purpose hanging around hoping to run into you does not qualify as stalking. Trust me, I'm a bit of an expert. I have the police report to prove it."

He had a hard time keeping his own eyebrows from shooting up. "You're a convicted stalker?"

Her laugh was quite a bit more amused this time. "Not yet. Don't go and ruin my perfect record now either, okay?" She shrugged and slipped off her sunglasses. "I picked up a stalker in Miami a couple of years ago. So I'm pretty familiar with American law. I would hope it's reasonably similar in Alma."

Sobering immediately, he tamped down the sudden and violent urge to punch whomever had threatened Bella's peace of mind. She'd mentioned it so casually, as if it wasn't a big deal, but it bloody well *was*. "What do you mean, you picked up a stalker? Like you went to the market to get milk and you just couldn't resist selecting a nutter to shadow you all the way home? No more jokes. Is he in jail?"

That may have come out a little more fiercely than he'd intended, but oh, well. He didn't take it back.

Wide-eyed, she shook her head. "He was practically harmless. A little zealous with his affections, maybe. I was out for the evening and he broke into my bedroom, where he waited for me to come home, bouquet of flowers in hand, like we were a couple. Or at least that was his sworn testimony. When my father found out, he immediately called the police, the mayor of Miami and the CEO of the company who'd sold him the security system installed on the grounds. I'm afraid they were rather harsh with the intruder."

Harmless? Anyone who could bypass a security system was far from harmless.

"As well they should have been." James developed an instant liking for Bella's obviously very level-headed father. "Was that the extent of it? Do I need to worry about the nutter following you across the pond?"

James had had his share of negative attention, invasions of privacy and downright hostile encounters with truly disturbed people. But he had fifty pounds and eight inches on Bella, plus he knew how to take care of himself. Bella was delicate and gorgeous and worthy of being treated like the princess she was. The thought of a creepy mouth-breather following her through the streets of Alma in hopes of doing depraved things made him furious.

"I doubt it. I haven't heard a peep from him in two years." She contemplated James with a small smile and crossed her arms over the angular sundress she wore. "You seem rather fierce all of a sudden. Worried about me?"

"Yes," he growled and shook his head. She was

not any of his concern—or at least she shouldn't be. "No. I'm sure your security is perfectly adequate."

He waved at the pair of ex-military types who waited a discreet distance away.

"Oh, yeah. My father insisted." Her nose wrinkled up delicately. "I'm pretty sure they're half security and half babysitters."

"Why do you need a babysitter?"

He couldn't leave it alone, could he? He should be bidding her good afternoon and running very fast in the other direction. But she constantly provoked his interest, and it was oh-so-deliberate. She wasn't walking away either and he'd bet it was because she felt the attraction sizzling between them just as much as he did.

Hell, everything he'd learned about her thus far indicated she liked the hint of naughtiness to their encounters…because they weren't supposed to be attracted to each other.

"I have a tendency to get into trouble." She waggled her brows. "These guys are here to keep me honest. Remind me that I have royal blood in my veins and a responsibility to the crown."

That was too good of a segue to pass up. "Really? What kind of trouble?"

"Oh, the worst kind," she stressed and reached out to stroke his arm in deliberate provocation. "If you've got a reputation to uphold, you'd best steer clear."

The contact of her nails on his bare arm sang through him. This was the most fun he'd had all day. "Sweetheart, I hate to disillusion you, but I've managed to ruin my reputation quite nicely all by my own self. Hanging out with you might actually improve it."

"Huh." She gave him a wholly inappropriate once-over that raised the temperature a few thousand degrees. "I'm dying to know. What did you do?"

"You really don't know?" That would be a first.

When she shook her head, he thought about glossing over it for a half second, but she'd find out soon enough anyway. "Mishap in Rio. Some unfortunate photographs starring me and a prostitute. I swear, money never came up, but there you go. The world didn't see it as an innocent mistake."

Gaze locked on his, she squeezed his arm. "Man after my own heart. Of all the things I thought we might have in common, that was not it. I'm recovering from my own photographer-in-the-bushes fiasco. Cretins."

"Oh, that's too bad. Sorry."

A moment of pure commiseration passed between them. And it spread into something dangerously affecting. They shared a complete lack of reverence for rules, their chemistry was off the charts and they were both in Alma trying to find their footing. It was practically criminal that he couldn't explore her gorgeous body and even more attractive mind to his heart's content.

But he couldn't. While he might have competed with Will over women in the past, this one was different. James wasn't in a good place to start anything with a woman anyway, especially not one who would live in the public eye for the foreseeable future. She needed to be with Will, who would take care of her and not sully her with failure.

Not to mention that his father seemed to have struck some kind of bargain with the Montoro family. Until James knew exactly what that entailed, he couldn't cross the line he so badly wanted to.

She'd flat out told him he'd have to be the strong

one, that he should stop tempting her. So that was the way it had to be.

James smiled and slipped his own sunglasses over his eyes so she couldn't read how difficult this was going to be for him. "Nice to see you again, Bella. I've got an appointment I'm late for so I've got to dash."

Casual. No commitment to calling her later. Exactly the right tone to brush her off.

She frowned and opened her mouth, but before she could say something they'd both likely regret, he added, "You should ring Will. Cheers," and whirled to take off down the boardwalk as fast he could.

Being noble tasted more bitter than he would have ever anticipated.

Three

James's rebuff stayed with Bella into the evening.

Apparently he wasn't of the same mind that a match between the Rowlings and Montoros could work just as easily between James and Bella as it could with his brother.

Being forced into a stiff, formal dinner with her father didn't improve her mood. Gabriel and Serafia were supposed to be there, too, which was the only reason Bella agreed, but the couple had yet to show.

Five bucks said they'd lost track of time while indulging in a much more pleasurable activity than dinner with Little Sister and Frosty Father. Lucky dogs.

Bella spooned up another bite of Marta's gazpacho, one of the best things the chef had prepared so far, and murmured her appreciation in case her father was actually paying attention to her today. But her mind was back on the boardwalk outside El Gatito. She'd have sworn the encounter with James would end with at least a kiss in the shadows of a storefront. Just to take the edge off until they got behind closed doors and let the simmering heat between them explode.

"Isabella." Her father's voice startled her out of an X-rated fantasy that she shouldn't have envisioned at all, let alone at the dinner table.

Not because of the X factor, but because it had starred James, who had cast her off with the lovely parting gift of his brother. *Call Will.* As if James had already grown tired of her and wanted to be clear about what her next steps should be.

"Yeah, Dad?" He must have realized that they were actually sitting at the same table. For once. She couldn't remember the last time they'd eaten together.

"You should know your great-aunt Isabella has decided to spend her last days in Alma. She arrived this morning and is asking after you."

Sudden happy tears burned Bella's eyelids. "Oh, that's the best news ever. Isn't she going to stay here with us?"

"The restoration of the monarchy is topmost on your aunt's mind." Rafael's gaze bored into her; he was no doubt trying to instill the gravity of royal protocol. "Therefore, she is staying in Del Sol. She wished to be close to El Castillo del Arena, so that she may be involved in Gabriel's coronation to the extent she is able."

Bella swore. Del Sol was, what? An hour away? Fine time to realize she should have taken her father up on the offer of a car…except she hadn't wanted to learn all the new traffic laws and Spanish road signs. Too late now—she'd have to take the chauffeured town car in order to visit Tía Isabella.

"Playa Del Onda is practically like Miami." Bella grumbled, mostly to herself. "You'd think she'd prefer the coast."

Her father put his spoon by his plate even though his bowl of gazpacho was still almost full. It hadn't been long enough since the last time they'd dined together for her to forget that meant a subject of grave importance was afoot and it wasn't her aunt's preference of locale.

"I have another matter to discuss. How was your first meeting with Will Rowling?"

Biting back a groan, she kept eating in a small show of defiance. Then she swallowed and said, "I haven't scheduled it yet."

Her father frowned. "I have it on good authority that you spoke to him today. On the boardwalk."

Spies? Her father had stooped to a new low. "I wasn't talking to Will. That was James."

Oh, duh. Her brand new security-guards-slash-babysitters had spilled the beans. Too bad they were the wrong beans.

Rafael's brows snapped together. "I cannot make myself more clear. Will Rowling is the man you should be pursuing."

Bella abandoned her spoon and plunked her elbows on the table to lean forward, so her father didn't miss her game face. "What if I like James better?"

Never mind that James had washed his hands of her. Regardless, it was the principle of the thing. Her father liked to try and run her life but failed to recall that Bella's typical response was to tell him to go to hell.

"James Rowling is bad news wrapped with trouble," Rafael shot back with a scowl. "He is not good enough for my daughter."

It seemed as if James had quoted this exact conversation to her yesterday on the beach. What was he, psychic? James's comment about the photographs that had gotten him into trouble crossed her mind and she realized there must be more to the story. She actually knew very little about the man other than the way he made her feel when he looked at her.

She eyed her father. What if Rafael had *told* James to brush her off? Would James have listened? She wouldn't put it past her father to interfere and now she wished she'd chased James down so she could ask. Shoot. She'd have to arrange another accidental meeting in order to find out.

"Maybe I'd like to make that decision on my own."

"Perhaps you need a few more facts if you're determined to undo the work I've already done on your behalf." Her father rubbed his graying temple. "Will Rowling is the next CEO of Rowling

Energy, and he will be of paramount importance to your brother's relationship with the entire European oil market. How do you suppose the Montoros will lead a country rich with oil if we do not have the appropriate alliances in place?"

"Gabriel's smart. He'll figure it out," she said, but it came out sounding a little sullen. As smart and capable as Gabriel may be, he'd never been king before and besides, Alma hadn't had a king in a long time, so her brother would be a bit of a trailblazer.

She owed it to Gabriel to give him a leg up.

"Have you given any thought to Will Rowling's feelings, Isabella? You haven't reached out to him in the three days since you've arrived. You could not have insulted him more if you tried."

No, she hadn't thought of that. She swore. Her father had a very small point. Miniscule. But a point nonetheless. How would she feel if Will had come to Miami to meet her and then didn't call her, choosing instead to flirt outrageously with her best friend, Nicole, for example?

She'd hunt Will down and tell him to his face what a dog he was. So why should she get a pass to do whatever pleased her? It didn't matter if her father had scared off James—this was about doing what she said she'd do.

"I'll meet Will. Tomorrow, if he's free," Bella promised and turned her attention to eating. The faster the gazpacho disappeared, the faster she could as well.

It didn't go down as well this time. Righteousness wasn't as fun as it looked in the brochure.

Will Rowling took Bella's call immediately, cleared his schedule for the next morning and agreed to take her on a tour of Alma. He'd been very pleasant on the phone, though his British accent sounded a bit too much like James's for her liking.

When Will picked her up at 10:30 a.m. on the dot, she flung the door open and actually had a bad Captain Obvious moment when she realized Will *looked* like James, too. *Duh.* As common as fraternal twins were among the moneyed set of Miami, she'd never actually met a set of identical twins.

She studied him for a long second, taking in the remarkable resemblance, until he cleared his throat and she found a dose of manners somewhere in her consciousness. "I'm so sorry! Hello. You must be Will."

"I don't know if I must be, but I am Will," he agreed.

Was that a joke? Trying not to be too obtrusive, she evaluated his expression but it was blank. With James, she never had to wonder. "I'm Bella, by the way."

"I assumed so. I have your picture."

Of course he did. And this was her house. Wasn't this fun? "Are you ready to go?"

"Yes, if you are." With a smile that didn't reach his eyes, he held out a hand toward his car, and waited until she left the house to follow her so he could help her into the passenger seat.

Will climbed into the driver's seat and buckled his seat belt carefully before starting the car, which guilted Bella into fastening hers as well. Seat belts. In an itty-bitty place like Alma, where nothing happened.

She sighed and pasted on a bright smile. "Safety first."

Usually she trotted that line out during a condom discussion. She almost cracked a joke along those lines, but something told her Will might not appreciate the parallel. Sinking down in her seat, she scouted for a topic of discussion. They were supposed to be seeing how they meshed, right?

Will must have had a similar thought process because he spoke first. "Thanks for arranging this, Bella. I'm chuffed to show you around Alma, but I'd like to know what you might be interested in seeing. Anything jump out at you? I'm at your command."

Did he mean that in the double-entendre way? A provocative rejoinder sprang to her lips that she'd have let fly if she'd been in the car with James. Should she flirt with Will, the way she normally did on a date, or would that just lead to him taking her up on it, when she wasn't even sure she wanted him to? Maybe she should just be herself, but what if Will hated her immediately? Would her father lay another guilt trip on her?

All of this second-guessing was making her nuts. She wasn't with James, and *everyone*—including James—wanted her to make nice with the proper Rowling. Yeah, she'd looked up James last night, finding far more information about him than she'd expected, and little of it would fit the definition of the word *proper*.

No one, not even James, had thought it relevant to mention the man was a professional soccer—*football* in Europe, apparently—player. Since he appeared to have quite a bit of fame, maybe he'd assumed she already knew. Regardless, bad press followed James around like it did her. No wonder her father had nearly had a heart attack when she mentioned James's name. He was the very opposite of the proper brother.

Proper pretty much covered Will's personality. Five minutes in, and judging by the stiff set of Will's shoulders, he wasn't as much of a fun time as his brother. Hopefully, she'd judged wrong and would soon discover otherwise.

"Thanks," she responded. "I've only seen the coast and a bit of Del Sol. Why don't you pick, since this is your home?"

"No problem." He shot her a small but pained smile, cluing her in that this whole set up might be as difficult for him as it was for her.

She should give him a break. "So, Will. How long have you lived in Alma?"

An innocuous enough subject, hopefully, and given the brothers' accents, it was a safe bet they hadn't been born here.

"Since I was seven. My father moved us here from England."

"Oh, that must have been quite an adventure."

She'd lived in Miami her whole life and living someplace new did have appeal for that reason alone. If only this arranged marriage business hadn't soured the experience of coming to Alma, she'd be having a blast. And that was why she still didn't think of it as her home... She still reserved the right to go back to Miami and play aunt instead of princess if the royal pressure grew too great.

Though with Tía Isabella's arrival in Alma, going home held much less appeal.

Will's face remained expressionless, but he tapped his pinky on the steering wheel in a staccato rhythm as he drove north out of Playa Del Onda along the coastal road that circled the main island.

"The move was difficult," he said shortly and paused so long, she wasn't sure he planned to continue. But then he said, "My mother had just died."

"I'm sorry," Bella murmured. "That *would* be difficult on young boys."

All at once, she realized this was James's history as well as Will's. And now she was absurdly interested in learning more. The gorgeous deep blues of the bay unfurled as far as the eye could see on her right but she ignored the spectacular view in favor of watching Will.

"Thanks." He glanced in the rearview mirror and double-checked the side mirrors before changing lanes. Will Rowling might very well be the most careful driver she'd ever met. "Look, let's just get all of it out on the table, shall we?"

"Depends on what you mean by *all* and *table*," she countered, a little puzzled by his abrupt change of subject.

Was this the part of the date where he expected her to air all her dirty laundry? She'd never had a long-term relationship, never wanted one, never thought about what went into establishing a foundation for one. Maybe they were supposed to spill deep, dark secrets right off the bat. She was *so* not on board with that.

"About the arranged marriage," he clarified. "We should clear the air."

"I'm not a lesbian looking for a fake husband and I don't have a crazy uncle chained up in the closet, if that's what you're fishing for."

He flashed a brief smile, the most genuine one

yet, giving her a glimpse of what he might be like if he loosened up a little. "I wasn't fishing. I meant, I wanted to tell you that marriage wasn't my idea. I'm not after your title or your fortune."

"Oh. Then what are you after?"

The smile vanished as his expression smoothed out into the careful nothingness he'd worn since the first moment. "Aligning myself with the Montoros through marriage is advantageous for Rowling Energy. It would be fitting if we suited each other. That's the only reason I agreed to meet you."

Ouch. That was kind of painful. Was she actually disappointed his motives for this pseudo-date nearly matched hers word for word? Well, not really, but no woman liked to find out a man was only interested in her connections. At least he'd admitted it up front.

All on the table, indeed.

"Yeah. I get that. My father pretty much insisted that I get on a plane and fall in love. Not necessarily in that order." Her lips twisted into a grimace automatically. "Since we're on the subject, would you really go through with it?"

"Marriage, you mean?" A shadow darkened his gaze though his eyes never left the road. "Rowling

Energy is on the brink of gaining a starring role on the world's oil stage. Our alliance makes very good sense. My assumption is that you thought so as well."

"Wow." Bella blinked. Had he memorized that careful statement in one sitting or had he repeated it to himself in the shower for the past week so he could get it out without stumbling? "I bet you say that to all the girls."

If she'd ever had any shred of doubt about her ability to tolerate an arranged marriage, it had just been crushed under the heel of Will's ambition. There was no way she'd marry *anyone* unless the words *deliriously happy, scorching passion* and *eternal love* entered into the conversation about a hundred times first, and even then, vows would be far, far in the future.

His eyebrows rose slightly. "Meaning?"

She rolled her eyes. "I just hadn't pegged you for a romantic. That's all."

"It wasn't intended to be romantic," he explained, and she had the distinct impression he really thought she'd needed the clarification.

As nightmare dates went, this one hit the scale

at about eleven point five. So much for being herself. *Check, please.*

"Will, I have a confession to make. Instead of seeing the sights, I'd really like a ride to Del Sol to visit my great-aunt Isabella." She blazed ahead before he could say no. "She's very sick and I'd like to see her. The timing is terrible, I realize, but my mind is just not where it should be for this outing."

Hitching a ride hadn't been her intent when she'd called him, but a savvy woman knew when to cut her losses and she might offend Will if she screamed bloody murder in his ear...which she might very well do if forced to spend five more minutes in his company.

This was not going to work out. Period. The last thing she wanted was to be stuck in a horrible marriage to a coldhearted man, as her mother had been. If it didn't make you happy, why do it? Why do *anything* that didn't have fun written all over it?

"No problem." Will checked forty-seven points of the car's position and did a U-turn to head to the interior of the island. "I sensed that you were distracted. Glad to know the reason why."

Yet another reason they would never work—obviously Will read her about as well as she could read Spanish. She'd been the opposite of distracted, but only because she'd been hoping for a scrap of information about James, God knew why.

"Yeah, I'm a mess. My aunt has Parkinson's and her prognosis is…not good." Bella left it at that and choked back the wave of emotion for a situation she couldn't change and hated with all her heart.

Good thing Will wasn't her type. Now she had the morning free to visit Tía Isabella and she didn't even have to feel guilty about it because she'd gone out with Will, as ordered.

"I'm sorry," Will said earnestly. "You should definitely visit her. We can go out another time when you're feeling more in the mood for company and conversation."

Oh, so *she* was the problem in this equation? She scowled but didn't comment because then she might say something she couldn't take back about the stick up Will's butt. "Sure. That would be nice."

"Well, this may be an ill-timed invitation, then, but Rowling Energy is throwing a party tonight at my father's house for some of our elite associates. Would you care to attend as my date? Might be less pressure and more fun than being one-on-one like this, trapped in a small car."

How…reasonable. Oh, sure it was strictly an opportunity for Will to trot her out around his snobby business partners who only cared about whom he knew. She wasn't stupid. But a party was right up her ally and the magic word *fun* only sweetened the pot. With enough champagne, she might even forget the whole setup reeked of royal responsibility and actually have a good time. Less pressure, as advertised.

Maybe she'd misjudged Will Rowling. "I have the perfect dress."

"It's settled, then."

In no time and with only one internet map miscalculation, they found Tía Isabella's narrow cobblestone street in the heart of Del Sol. Like a true gentleman, Will helped Bella from the car at the door of her great aunt's rental house, and had a word with Tía Isabella's housekeeper to ensure Bella would have a return ride home. The housekeeper promised to have a car sent from Playa Del Onda, so Will took his leave.

All in all, Will seemed like a nice, upstanding guy. He was certainly handsome enough and had gorgeous aqua-colored eyes. Too bad she couldn't get the sexier, more exciting version she'd tripped over at the beach off her mind.

"Patrick James Rowling!"

James groaned and thought about ducking out the door of the sunroom and escaping Casa Rowling through the back gate. When his father three-named him, the outcome was never fun nor in his favor.

Actually, any time his father spoke to him it was unpleasant. Even being in the same room with Patrick Rowling reminded James that his mother was dead and it was his father's fault. Time healed all wounds—except the ones that never should have happened in the first place. If his father hadn't yelled at his mum, she wouldn't have left in tears that night back in Guildford. Then his mum's single-car accident would never have happened. He and Will wouldn't have become motherless seven-year-old boys. The fractured Rowling family wouldn't have subsequently moved to Alma, where James didn't know anyone but Will, who was too shell-shocked to do anything other than mumble for nearly a year.

But all of that had happened and James would never forgive *or* forget.

As a result, James and Patrick gave each other a wide berth by mutual unspoken agreement, but it was harder to do when under the same roof. James should really get his own place, but he still wasn't sure if he planned to stay in Alma, so here he was.

Patrick Rowling, the man who'd named his first born after himself in a moment of pure narcissism, stormed into the sunroom and shoved a newspaper at James's chest with a great deal more force than necessary. "Explain this."

"This is commonly known as a newspaper." James drew out the syllables, ladening them with as much sarcasm as possible. "Many civilized nations employ this archaic method of communicating information and events to subscribers. Shall I delve into the finer points of journalism, or are we square on the purpose of this news vehicle?"

His father's face had grown a deeper, more satisfying shade of purple the longer James baited him. A thing of beauty. James moved his half-empty teacup out of the line of fire, in case of imminent explosion. It was Darjeeling and brewed perfectly.

"You can dispense with the smartass attitude.

I've had more than enough of it from you to last a lifetime."

What he really meant was that he'd had enough of James doing the opposite of what Patrick commanded. But if James toed the line, how could he make his father pay for his sins? Of course, his father could never truly pay in a lifetime. The sad part was that James might have settled for an apology from his father for all the horrible things he'd caused. Or at least a confession. Instead, his father heaped praises on Will the Perfect Son and generally pretended James didn't exist.

Until James managed to get his attention by doing something beyond the pale. Like whatever had gotten the elder Rowling's dander up this time.

His father poked the paper again. "There's a rather risqué photo of you on the front page. Normally, I would brush it off as further proof you care nothing for propriety and only your own self-destruction. But as it's a photo of you with your brother's fiancée, I find it impossible to ignore."

"What?" His brother had a *fiancée*? "What are you talking about?"

James shoved his father's hand away and shifted the paper so he could see the front page. There it was, in full color. He whistled. What a gorgeous shot of Bella in his arms. Her hair all mussed and legs tangled in his. He might have to cut it out and frame it.

Wait… *Bella* was Will's fiancée? This was news to James. Last he'd heard, Bella planned to see how things went before committing to marriage. Had Will even *met* Bella yet?

"Your timing is impeccable, as always. Now that we're all caught up, please explain how you managed to create a scandal so quickly." Dear old Dad crossed his arms over the paunch he liked to pretend gave him a stately demeanor, but in reality, only made him look dumpy.

Obviously they were nowhere near caught up.

"Maybe that's Will—did you ever think of that?" James challenged mildly and went back to sipping his tea because he had a feeling he'd need the fortification.

"Your brother is with the Montoro princess as we speak and it's their first meeting."

Montoro princess. Really? James rolled his eyes. His father couldn't be more pretentious if he tried. "If they hadn't even met until today, how are they already engaged?"

Waving his hand with a snort, Patrick gave him a withering look. "Merely a formality. They will be engaged, mark my words. So as far as you're concerned, she's your brother's fiancée. Will is quite determined to woo her and I've never seen him fail at anything he set his mind to."

Despite what should be good news—his father had deliberately thrown the word *fiancée* in James's face even though it wasn't true—James's gut twisted at the thought of Will and Bella together. Why, he couldn't explain, when he'd been the one to suggest Bella should ring Will. Obviously, she'd taken his advice and rather quickly, too. He'd just run into her in town yesterday.

"Smashing. I hope they're having a fantastic time and fall madly in love so they can give you lots of royal babies, since that's the most important accomplishment a Rowling could hope to achieve." The sentiment had started out sincerely but halfway through, disappointment had tilted his mood. James lived his life with few regrets but stepping aside so Will had a fair shot with Bella ranked as a decision he'd questioned more than once.

"Don't change the subject. If you deliberately staged that picture with the princess to ruin your brother's chances, the consequences will be dire," his father warned.

James couldn't quite bite back the laugh that burst out. "Oh, please, no. Perhaps you'll disown me?"

What else could his father possibly do to him besides constantly express his displeasure in everything James did? Being signed with Real Madrid hadn't rated a mention. Being named captain of the Alma World Cup team wasn't worthy enough of a feat to get a comment.

Oh, but miss a goal—that had earned James an earful.

Patrick leaned forward, shoving his nose into James's space and into his business all at the same time. "If you don't stay away from the Montoro princess, I will personally ensure you never play football again."

James scoffed. "You're off your trolley. You have no power in my world."

And neither did James, not now. It pricked at his temper that his father would choose that method to strike at him. Patrick clearly failed to comprehend his son's life crisis if he didn't already know that James had managed to thoroughly subvert his own career with no help from anyone.

The threat gave him a perverse desire to prove he could come back from the twin failures of a missed goal and a dropped contract. He needed to play, if for no other reason than to show everyone James Rowling couldn't be kept down.

"Perhaps. Do you want to wager on that?"

James waved nonchalantly with one hand and clenched the other into a tight fist. What colossal nerve. A supreme act of will kept the fist in his lap, though letting it fly against the nearby wall might have ended the conversation quite effectively.

"Seems like pretty good odds to me, so don't be surprised if I roll the dice with Bella." He waggled his brows. "I think that picture is enough of an indicator that she fancies me, don't you think?"

Which might have been true when the picture was snapped, but probably wasn't now that he'd stepped aside. Will would be his charming self and Bella would realize that she could have the best of both worlds—the "right" Rowling and her father's blessing. Probably better for everyone, all the way around.

Deep down, James didn't believe that in the

slightest. He and Bella had a spark between them, which wouldn't vanish with a hundred warnings from the old geezer.

"The monarchy is in its fledgling stages." Patrick hesitated for the first time since barging into the sunroom and James got the impression he was choosing his words carefully. "Rowling Energy has a unique opportunity to solidify our allegiance and favor through the tie of marriage. There is only one Montoro princess."

"And only one heir to the company," James said sourly. "I get it. Will's the only one good enough for her."

His father sighed. The weariness that carved lines into his face around his mouth had aged him quickly and added a vulnerability to his expression that James hadn't been prepared for. Patrick had never been anything other than formidable for as long as James could remember.

"I would welcome you at Rowling Energy if you expressed but a smidgen of determination and interest." Then his father hardened back into the corporate stooge he'd become since entering into the high stakes oil market. Dad had too many zeroes in his bank account balance to truly be in touch with his humanity. "Will has done both, with remarkable success. If you would think of someone other than yourself, you'd realize that Will has much to gain from this alliance. I will not be at the helm of Rowling forever. Will needs every advantage."

Guilt. The best weapon. And it might have worked if James truly believed all that drivel. Marrying into the royal family was about his father's ambition, not Will's.

"Maybe we should let Bella sort it on her own, eh?" James suggested mildly. He didn't mind losing to Will, as long as the contest was fair.

"There's nothing to sort," his father thundered, growing purple again. "Stay away from her. Period. No more risqué pictures. No more contact. Do not ruin this for your brother."

To put the cap on his mandate, Patrick Rowling stormed from the sun-room in much the same manner as he entered it. Except now Bella Montoro had been transformed into the ripest forbidden fruit.

James had never met a scandal he didn't want to dive headlong into, especially when it involved a gorgeous woman who clearly had the hots for him. Pissing his father off at the same time James introduced himself to the pleasures of Princess Bella was just a sweet bonus.

Four

Bella spent two wonderful hours catching up with her great aunt Isabella, but the sickly woman grew tired so easily. Coupled with the fact that Isabella's advanced Parkinson's disease meant she was bedridden, it was difficult for Bella to witness her once-vibrant aunt in this condition. Regardless, she kept a bright smile pasted on throughout their visit.

But even Bella could see it was time for her to leave lest she overtire Isabella.

Before she asked her aunt's nurse to call a cab, Bella took Isabella's hand and brought it to her cheek. "I'm glad you decided to come to Alma."

"This is where I choose to die," Isabella said simply with a half smile, the only facial expression she could still muster. "I will see Gabriel become king and my life will be complete."

"I wish you wouldn't say things like that."

It was depressing and wretched to think of the world spinning on without Isabella, whom Bella loved unconditionally and vice versa. Her throat burned with grief and unreconciled anger over a circumstance she couldn't change.

Geez, she'd been less upset when her mother had left. That had at least made sense. Parkinson's disease did not.

"It is but truth. All of us must make our lives what we can in the time allotted to us." Isabella paused, her voice catching. "Tell me. Have you visited the farmhouse yet?"

"What farmhouse?" Had her father mentioned something about a farmhouse and she'd been too busy ignoring him to remember? Shoot. She'd have done anything Isabella asked, even if the request came via her father.

"Oh, dear." Her aunt closed her eyes for a moment. "No, I don't believe I imagined it. It's white. In the country. Aldeia Dormer. Very important. My mother told me and Rafael of it. My brother is gone, God rest his soul, so I'm telling you. You must find it and…"

Trailing off with a blank expression, Isabella sat silent for a moment, her hand shaking uncontrollably inside Bella's as it often had even before her aunt's disease had progressed to include forgetfulness and the inability to walk.

"I'll find the farmhouse," Bella promised. "What should I do when I find it?"

"The countryside is lovely in the spring," her aunt said with bright cheer. "You take your young man with you and enjoy the ride."

"Yes, ma'am." Bella smiled. Wouldn't it be nice to actually have a "young man" in the sweet, old-fashioned sense that Isabella had meant? Bella had only mentioned Will because her father had apparently told Isabella all about the stupid arranged marriage. It was the first thing her aunt had asked after.

"Wear a red dress to the party tonight and take photographs." Isabella closed her eyes and just when Bella thought she'd fallen asleep, she murmured, "Remember we all have a responsibility to our blood. And to Alma. I wish Rafael could be here to see his grandson take the throne."

"Red dress it is," Bella said, skipping over the royal responsibility part because she'd had enough of that for a lifetime.

Wasn't it enough that she was going to the party as Will's date when she'd rather be meeting James there? And if James happened to show, would it be so much of a crime if she danced with him once or twice? She'd still be Will's date, just the way everyone wanted, but would also give herself the opportunity to find out if James had pawned her off on his brother because he didn't like her or because of some other reason.

Guilt cramped her stomach as her aunt remained silent. Yeah, so maybe Bella considered it a possible bonus that she might run into James at the party. Was that so bad?

"Isabella, I—" Bella bit her lip before she spilled all her angst and doubt over what her father had asked her to do by giving Will a chance. Her aunt was tired and didn't need to be burdened with Bella's problems.

"The farmhouse. It's part of the Montoro legacy, passed down from the original Rafael Montoro I, to his son Rafael II. And then to his son

Rafael III. Remember the farmhouse, child," her aunt wheezed out in the pause.

"I will." Before she could change her mind again, Bella went for broke. "But I might take a different young man with me than the one my father wants me to marry. Would that be a bad thing?"

"You must make your own choices," her aunt advised softly. "But beware. All choices have consequences. Be sure you are prepared to face them."

Isabella's shaking hand went slack as she slipped off into sleep for real this time. Bella took her leave reluctantly and slid into the waiting car her father had sent for her, wishing her aunt wasn't so sick that they could only have half of a conversation.

What had Isabella meant by her warning? During the hour-long ride back to Playa Del Onda, Bella grappled with it. Unfortunately, she had a sinking feeling she knew precisely what her aunt had been attempting to tell her. Being born during a hurricane hadn't infused Bella with a curse that meant she'd always leave broken hearts in her wake. It was her own decisions that had consequences, and if she wanted to be a better person than she'd been in Miami, she had to make different, more conscious choices.

Hurricane Bella couldn't cut a swath through Alma, leaving broken pieces of her brother's reign in her wake. Or broken pieces of her father's agreement with Will's father. Mentioning all of Bella's ancestors hadn't been an accident—Isabella wanted her to remember her roots.

Either she had try for real with Will and then tell him firmly it wasn't going to work, or she had to skip the party. It wasn't fair to anyone to go with the intention of running into James for any reason.

By the time the party rolled around, Bella was second-guessing the red dress. She'd never worn it before but distinctly remembered loving it when she'd tried it on at the boutique in Bal Harbour. Now that she had it on…the plunging neckline and high slit in the skirt revealed a shocking amount of flesh. But she'd promised Isabella she'd wear red, and it was too late to find another dress.

And honestly, she looked divine in it, so… Sexy red dress got the thumbs up. If she and Will were going to get along, he'd have to accept that she liked to feel beautiful in what she wore. This dress filled the bill. And then some. If a neckline that plunged all the way to the dress's waistband caused a problem with Rowling's business associates, better she and Will both find out now they weren't a good match.

The chauffeur helped her into the back of the Montoro car. Thankfully, Will hadn't offered to pick her up so she had an easy escape if need be. *Please God, don't let me need an escape.*

Within ten minutes, the car had joined the line of Bentleys, Jaguars and limousines inching their way to the front steps of the Rowling mansion. Like the Montoros' house, the Rowlings' Playa Del Onda residence overlooked the bay. She smiled at the lovely sight of the darkened water dotted with lighted boats.

When Bella entered the double front doors, Will approached her immediately, as if he'd been waiting for her. His pleasant but slightly blank expression from earlier was still firmly in place and she bit back a groan. How long were they going to act like polite strangers?

Jaw set firmly, Will never glanced below her shoulders. Which sort of defeated the purpose of such a racy dress. What was the point of showing half her torso if a man wasn't even going to look at it?

"Bella, so nice to see you again," Will murmured and handed her a champagne flute. "That dress is stunning."

Okay, he'd just earned back all the points that he'd lost. "Thanks. Nice to see you, too."

His tuxedo, clearly custom-cut and very European, gave him a sophisticated look that set him slightly apart from the other male guests, most of whom were older and more portly. Will was easy on the eyes and commanded himself with confidence. She could do worse.

Will cleared his throat. "Did you have a nice afternoon?"

"Yes. You?"

"Dandy."

She sipped her champagne as the conversation ground to a halt. Painfully. Gah, normally she thrived on conversation and loved exchanging observations, jokes, witty repartee. Something.

The hushed crowd murmured around them and the tinkle of chamber music floated between the snippets of dialogue, some in English, some in Spanish. Or Portuguese. Bella still couldn't tell the difference between the two despite hearing Spanish spoken by Miami residents of Cuban descent for most of her life.

She spotted her cousin Juan Carlos Salazar across the room and nearly groaned. While they'd grown up together after his parents died, he'd always been too serious. Why wasn't he in Del Sol managing something?

Of course, he looked up at that moment and their gazes met. He wove through the crowd to clasp Will's hand and murmur his appreciation for the party to his hosts. Juan Carlos was the kind of guy who always did the right thing and at the same time, made everyone else look as if they were doing the wrong thing. It was a skill.

"Bella, are you enjoying the party?" he asked politely.

"Very much," she lied, just as politely because she had skills, too, just not any that Juan Carlos would appreciate. "I saw Tía Isabella. I'm so glad she decided to come to Alma."

"I am as well. Though she probably shouldn't be traveling." Juan Carlos frowned over his grandmother's stubbornness, which Bella had always thought was one of her best traits. "Uncle Rafael tried to talk her out of it but she insisted."

The Montoros all had a stubborn streak but Bella's father took the cake. Time for a new subject. "How are things in the finance business?"

"Very well, thank you." He shot Will a cryptic glance. "Better now that you're in Alma working toward important alliances."

She kept her eyes from rolling. Barely. "Yes, let's hear it for alliances."

Juan Carlos and Will launched into a conversation with too many five-syllable words for normal humans to understand, so Bella amused herself by scrutinizing Will as he talked, hoping to gather more clues about his real personality.

As he spoke to Juan Carlos, his attention wandered, and Bella watched him watch a diminutive dark-haired woman in serviceable gray exit by a side door well away from the partygoers. An unfamiliar snap in Will's gaze had her wondering who the woman was. Or rather, who she was to Will. The woman's dress clearly marked her as the help.

Will didn't even seem to notice when Juan Carlos excused himself.

"Do you need to attend to a problem with the servants?" Bella inquired politely.

She'd gone to enough of her parents' parties to

know that a good host kept one eye on the buffet and the other on the bar. Which was why she liked attending parties, not throwing them.

"No. No problem," Will said grimly and forced his gaze back to Bella's face. But his mind was clearly elsewhere.

Which told her quite a bit more about the situation than Will probably intended. Perhaps the dark-haired woman represented at least a partial answer for why Will seemed both pained by Bella's presence and alternatively agreeable to a marriage of convenience.

Bella had come to the party as requested by God and everyone and she deserved a chance with Will. He owed it to her, regardless of whether he had something going on with the diminutive maid.

"Look, Will—"

"Let's dance." He grabbed her hand and led her to the dance floor without waiting for an answer, off-loading their champagne glasses onto a waiter's tray as they passed by.

Okay, then. Dancing happened to be one of her favorite things about parties, along with dressing up and laughing in a private corner with someone she planned to let strip her naked afterward.

For some reason, the thought of getting naked with Will made her skin crawl. Two out of three wasn't bad, though, was it?

The quartet seated in the corner had switched from chamber music to a slightly less boring bossa nova–inspired piece. Not great, but she had half a chance of finding a groove at least.

Was this how the people of Alma partied? Or had the glitzy Miami social scene spoiled her? Surely not. Alma was one of the wealthiest countries in the European Union. What was she missing?

Halfway into the song, Will had yet to say a word and his impersonal hand at her waist might as well have belonged to an eighty-year-old grandfather. This might go down in history as the first time a man under thirty had danced with her and not used it as an excuse to pull her into his strong embrace. It was as if Will had actually wanted to *dance* or something.

None of this screamed, "I'm into you."

Perhaps the problem with this party lay with the host, not the country. Will might need a little encouragement to loosen up.

When the interminably long dance finally ended,

Bella smiled and fanned herself as if she'd grown overheated. "My, it's a little warm in here."

Will nodded. "I'll get you another glass of champagne."

Before he could disappear, she stopped him with a hand on his arm, deliberately leaning into it to make the point. "That's okay. Let's go out on the terrace and talk."

The whole point was to get to know each other. The car trip hadn't worked. Dancing hadn't worked. They needed to try something else.

"Maybe in a few minutes," Will said with a glance around the room at large. "After I've played the proper host."

Disappointment pulled at her mouth but she refused to let a frown ruin her lipstick. "I hope you won't mind if I escape the heat for a bit by myself."

For a moment, she wondered if he'd really let her go. He'd invited her, after all, and hadn't introduced her to one person yet. This was supposed to be a date, wasn't it?

"Certainly." Will inclined his head toward the double glass doors off the great room. "I'll find you later."

Fuming, Bella wound through the guests to the

terrace—by herself!—and wondered when she'd lost her edge. Clearly a secluded terrace with a blonde American in half a dress didn't appeal to Will Rowling. What did—dark-haired housekeepers?

Great, she thought sourly. Bella had come to the party with the genuine intent of seeing where things might go with Will, because she said she would. Because she'd bought into the hoopla of being a princess, which came with responsibilities she'd never asked for nor wanted any part of.

But she'd done it, only to be hit over the head with the brutal truth yet again. The man her father wanted her to marry had less than zero interest in her as a person. She wouldn't be surprised to learn Will was perfectly okay with a hard-core marriage of convenience, complete with separate bedrooms and a paramour on the side.

Sounded an awful lot like her parents' marriage, and *that* she wanted no part of.

She shuddered, despondent all at once. Was it asking too much for someone to care what she would actually have to sacrifice with this mess her father had created?

The night was breathtaking, studded with stars

and a crescent moon. Still, half the stone terrace lay in shadow, which went perfectly with her mood. Leaning on the railing, she glanced down into the crash of ocean against the cliff below.

"Thinking of jumping?"

The male voice emanating from behind her skittered down her spine, washing her in a myriad of emotions as her heart rolled and her pulse quickened. But she didn't turn to face him because she was afraid if she actually glimpsed James for even a fraction of a second, all of her steely resolve to work things out with his brother would melt like gelato in the sun. And the leftover hot sticky mess would be difficult to clean up indeed.

"Would you stop me?" she murmured.

"No. I'd hold your hand all the way down, though."

Her eyelids fluttered closed. How had he managed to make that sound so daringly romantic?

The atmosphere shifted as he moved closer. She could feel him behind her, hear the intake of his breath. A sense of anticipation grew in the silence, peppering her skin with goose pimples and awareness.

Before it grew too intense, she blurted out, "I called Will."

James wasn't for her. She needed to keep reminding herself that.

"I gathered that." He sounded amused and reckless simultaneously. "I plan to personally drive him to the eye doctor tomorrow."

"Oh? Is he having problems with his eyes?"

"Obviously. Only a blind man would let you out of his sight, especially if he knew you planned to be alone on a moonlit terrace. Any plonker could be out here, waiting to ravish you."

She'd been so wrong. Other than a similar accent, James's voice was nothing like Will's. Will had yet to lose the ice while James breathed pure fire when he spoke.

"Good thing his moral, upstanding brother is the only one out here. He wouldn't dare lay a finger on me."

Maybe James needed a reminder that Bella and Will were supposed to get married, too. After all James had been the one to cool things off between the two of them, which had absolutely been the right thing to do.

"Yeah? While Will's having his eyes examined,

maybe I'll get my IQ checked, then," James said silkily.

"Feeling a little brainless this evening?"

"I definitely feel like my brain has turned to mush. I think it's that dress. Your bare back framed by that little bit of fabric…it makes me imagine all sorts of things that probably aren't very smart." The frank appreciation in his voice floated through the still night, wrapping around her deliciously. "Let me see the front."

"No." Feeling exposed all at once, she crossed her arms. "I didn't wear this dress for you."

"Shame. I'm the only one here who fully appreciates what's underneath it."

In a flash, her core heated with the memory of being in James's arms on the beach, his hard body flush with hers.

"You shouldn't speak to me like that," she said primly, and nearly gasped as he drew achingly close to her back. She could sense his heat and it called to her.

"Because you don't like it?" he murmured, his mouth not two inches from her ear in a deliberate tease that shot sensation down the back of her throat.

Her breath caught and she gripped the railing lest her weak knees give out. "Because I do."

He laughed and it spiked through her with fingers of warmth.

"That's right," he said smoothly, as if recalling something critically important. "You're weak and liable to give in to temptation. Everything I've always wanted in a woman."

"That's so funny. I'd swear you brushed me off at our last meeting," she couldn't help but reply. It still stung, despite all the reasons why she suspected he'd done so.

"I did," he admitted in an unprecedented moment of honesty. Most men she'd ever met would have tried to pass it off, as if she'd been mistaken. "You know why."

"Because you're not interested."

The colorful curse he muttered made her smile for some reason. "You need *your* IQ checked if you believe that."

"Because my father scared you off?"

"Not even close."

"Because I'm supposed to be with Will," she said definitively and wished it hadn't come out sounding so bitter.

"Yes." James paused as if to let that sink in. "Trust me. It was not easy. But he's my brother."

"So you're okay with it if I marry Will?"

She imagined Christmas. That would be fun, to sit next to her boring husband who was screwing another woman on the side while the man she'd been dreaming about sat across the room. As Mr. Rowling carved the turkey, she could bask in the warm knowledge that she'd furthered a bunch of male ambition with her sacrifice to the royal cause.

"Is that what you want?" he asked quietly, his voice floating out on the still night air.

The question startled her. She had a choice. Of course she did. And now she needed to make it, once and for all.

The night seemed to hold its breath as it waited for her to speak. This was it, the moment of truth. She could end this dangerous attraction to the wrong brother forever by simply saying yes. James would walk away.

Something shifted inside, warring with all the sermons on responsibility and family obligations. And she couldn't stand it any longer.

She didn't want Will.

Whirling, she faced James, greedily drinking

him, cataloguing the subtle differences in his features. He and Will weren't identical, not to her. The variances were in the way James looked at her, the way her body reacted. The heat in this man's gaze couldn't be mistaken. He was all James and 100 percent the object of her desire.

She let her gaze travel over his gorgeous body, clad in a tuxedo that fit like an extension of his skin, fluid and beautiful. And she wanted nothing more than to see the secrets it hid so carefully beneath the fabric.

He raked her with a once-over in kind that quickened her core with delicious tightness. *That* was how a man should look at you in such a dress. As if he'd been presented with every last fantasy in one package.

"The back was good," he rasped, his voice clogged with undisguised desire. "But the front…"

Delighted that she'd complied with Isabella's fortuitous request to wear red, she smiled. "I do like a man at a loss for words."

Moonlight played over his features and glinted off the obscenely expensive watch on his wrist as he swept up her hand and drew her closer. So close, she could almost hear his heart beating.

"Actions speak louder and all that." His arm slid around her waist, pulling her to within a hairsbreadth of his body and she ached for him to close the distance. "Plus, I didn't want to miss your answer."

"Answer to what?"

He lowered his head to murmur in her ear, "What it is that you want."

If she wanted Will, Bella had about two seconds to say so, or James would be presenting the woman in his arms with some hot and heavy temptation. He preferred to get on the same page before that happened because he had a bad feeling *he* might be the weak one on this terrace.

With so much forbidden fruit decked out in a mouthwatering dress that screamed sin and sex, he'd rather not put his ability to resist Bella to the test. But he would resist if she said no, regardless of whether he'd been baiting her in hopes of getting her to break first. Because then he'd be in the clear if she came on to him, right?

The sharp intake of her breath and a sensuous lift of her lips gave him all the nonverbal communication he needed. Then she put the icing on it with a succinct, "Will who?"

The gap between their bodies slowly vanished until their torsos brushed, but he couldn't have said if he closed it or she did. This was not what he'd planned when Bella had inadvertently joined him on the terrace, but it was certainly what he'd fantasized might happen if she'd given him the slightest encouragement.

With her lithe little body teasing his, her curves scarcely contained by that outrageous dress, he could hardly get his mind in gear long enough to form complete sentences. "You could have just said that from the outset."

"You could have said *call me instead of Will* on the boardwalk."

Not if he'd hoped to sleep at night he couldn't have. Of course, he'd done little of that anyway, tossing and turning as he imagined this gorgeous, vibrant woman with his brother.

He nodded in concession, hardly breathing for fear of alerting her to how very turned on he was. "It was my one noble gesture for the decade. Don't expect another one."

She laughed and he felt it vibrate against his

rock-hard lower half, which did not improve matters down below. Dangerous and forbidden did it for him in the worst way and when both came in a package like Bella, he might as well surrender to the moment right now. They were both aware of where this was headed, weren't they?

"You know, you spend a lot of time blabbing about how wicked you are, but I've yet to see evidence of it." Her brow arched saucily, turning silvery in the moonlight. "What happened to my man of action?"

"You wanna play?" he growled and slid his hand to the small of her back, pushing her deep into the crevices of his body. "Here's round one of How Bad Can James Be?"

Tipping up her head, he captured her smart mouth with his lips, molding them shut while tasting her simultaneously. What started as a shut-up kiss instantly transformed, becoming slow and sensuous and exploratory as he delved into her sweetness. She met him stroke for stroke, angle for angle, silently begging him to take her deeper.

He *finally* had Bella in his arms. Exactly as he'd ached to have her since releasing her from their first embrace.

Still in the throes of an amazing kiss he never wanted to end, he pinned her against the stone railing, wedging their bodies tight and leaving his hands free to roam where they pleased.

And that creamy expanse of flesh from neck to waist had been calling his name for an eternity. Almost groaning with the pleasure of her mouth under his, he slid a palm north to let his fingertips familiarize themselves with her bare back. Heated, smooth flesh greeted his touch. Greedily, he caressed it all and she moaned throatily, flattening her back against his palm, pleading for more.

He gave it to her.

Nearly mindless with the scent of Bella filling his head, he held her closer in his arms, sliding a knee between her legs to rub at her sweet spot. Heavenly. He wanted to touch every part of her, to taste what he'd touched. To take them both to nirvana again and again as the blistering, forbidden attraction between them was allowed free reign once and for all.

Suddenly, she tore her mouth free and moved out of reach, breathing heavily. "That was…um—"

"Yeah." Earthshaking. Unprecedented. Hotter

than Brazil in the summer. "Come back so I can do it again."

He reached for her and for a second, he thought she was going to do it. Her body swayed toward him and his mouth tingled in anticipation of locking on to those lips of hers again.

But then she shook her head, backing up another step. "I can't be with you like this. It's not fair to Will. We have to straighten everything out first."

Bloody hell. Will hadn't crossed his mind once while James kissed his brother's date. Any of dear Father's business cronies could have come upon them on the terrace and there were few people in Alma who confused the twins. Everyone knew James had inherited Grandfather Rowling's priceless antique watch—much to Patrick's chagrin. It was the first thing people looked for when in need of a handy way to identify the brothers.

"Yes, of course you're right." Though his body ached to yank her back into his arms, he gave her a pained smile instead. "This isn't over."

"Oh, no." She shot him an indecipherable look. "Not by half. The next time you and I are together, I will be naked and screaming your name."

His eyelids flew shut and he groaned. "Why can't that happen tonight?"

"Because as far as the rest of the world is concerned, Will is the Rowling I'm supposed to be with. I've had too many scandals mess up my life to knowingly create a preventable one. That's why it must be perfectly clear to everyone that Will and I are not getting married before you and I get naked."

Grimly, he nodded, the photo of the two of them on the front page fresh in his mind. They should probably address that, too, at some point, but he'd topped out on issues he could reasonably deal with.

"You should go. And go fast before I change my mind." Or lose it. "I'm fresh out of nobility *and* the capacity to resist you."

She whirled and fled. He watched her beautiful back as she disappeared inside the house, and then went in search of a bottle of Jameson to get him through what promised to be a long night indeed.

Five

James cornered Will in his Rowling Energy office at 9:05 a.m. This was the earliest James could recall being awake, dressed and out of the house in quite some time. But this cat-and-mouse game had grown tiresome, and the man who shared his last name, his blood and once upon a time, had even shared a womb, had the power to end it.

"Will."

James didn't cross the threshold out of respect for the fact that he was on his brother's turf. Instead, he waited for him to glance up from his report. Will's expression remained composed, though James caught a flash of surprise in the depths of his gaze, which the Master of Calm quickly banked.

"Yes?"

And now they'd officially exchanged two words this week. Actually, James couldn't remember the last time they *had* talked. They'd never been close. Hell, they were rarely on the same continent, but that wasn't really the reason. The divide had started the night their mum died and grown exponentially over the years.

"We have to talk. Can I come in?"

"Since you're here already, I suppose." Will's long-suffering sigh said he deserved a medal for seeing James on such short notice.

James bit back the sarcasm strictly because he was the one with the mission, though his brother's condescension pricked at his temper. The brothers would never see eye to eye, though why James cared was beyond him.

They'd taken different paths in dealing with the single most defining year of their lives, Will choosing to compensate for the loss of everything familiar by becoming whatever their father said, as long as the remaining parent paid attention to him.

James compensated for his mother's death by

lashing out at his father, refusing to forgive the ultimate crime—though James could never run far enough or get into enough trouble to drown out the sound of his own conscience. While he'd never forgive his father for driving his mum out into the rainy night, back in the deepest reaches of his soul, he blamed himself more.

Because he'd heard them arguing and hadn't done anything. What if he'd run out of his hiding place to grab on to his mum and beg her not to leave? She wouldn't have. He knew she wouldn't have. But she'd probably assumed both her boys were asleep. One of them had been.

James took a deep, not at all calming breath as he settled into one of the wingback chairs flanking Will's desk. "It's about Bella."

"Ms. Montoro? What about her?"

James rolled his eyes. "Well, I was going to ask how serious you are about her, but that pretty much told me."

"How serious I…" Will's gaze narrowed. "You've got the hots for her."

That didn't begin to describe what had happened on the terrace last night. Or every moment since the princess had blinked up at him with those big

eyes after upending his world. "If you're determined to see this arranged marriage through, I
won't stand in your way."

Steepling his hands, Will sat back in his chair,
contemplating James carefully. "Really? That's a
first."

"What's that supposed to mean?"

"When was the last time you considered anyone above yourself? Especially when a woman is
involved."

James was halfway out of his seat before he
checked himself. Fisting his hand in his lap as he
sat back down, he forced a smile. "I won't apologize for looking out for myself. No one else does.
But I will concede the point. This woman is different."

He nearly choked on the words he hadn't consciously planned to say. But it was true. Bella
wasn't like anyone else he'd ever met.

Smirking, Will nodded once. "Because she's earmarked for me."

Is that what he thought this was about? That
James had come to Will in a fit of jealousy?

"Earmarked? Is that how you talk about her?
Bella's a person, not a pile of money."

The nerve. Will had spent too much time in budget meetings if he equated a flesh-and-blood woman with reserve funds.

"Yes. But surely you realize we're talking about an arranged marriage. It's a form of currency, dating back to the dawn of time. No one is under a different impression."

James had a sick sort of realization that what Will described was probably quite right. Two fathers had struck a deal, bargaining away their children's future with no thought to what could or should go into a marriage decision. Namely, the desires of the bride and groom in question.

If he didn't miss his guess, Will accepted that. Embraced it. Thought it was a brilliant idea.

If James had known this was the case, he'd have taken Bella straight to his room last night and skipped the formality of giving his brother a heads-up that things had changed. "Bella has a different impression. She's not interested in being bought *or* sold."

Will eyed him thoughtfully. "Why hasn't she come to me herself?"

"Because this is between you and me, brother. She didn't want to get into the middle of it." Which he fully appreciated, whether Will did or not. James had to look at himself in the mirror for the rest of his life and he'd prefer not to see his own guilty conscience staring back at him. "And she won't. Neither will I allow her to. If you say you're planning to pursue this ridiculous idea of aligning Rowling Energy to the Montoros through marriage, so be it. Just be sure you treat her like a princess."

Maybe James wasn't done being noble after all. He'd fully expected to walk in here and demand that Will release Bella from their fathers' agreement. But somehow he'd wound up caring more about Bella and how she was being marginalized than whether he'd cleared the way to sleep with her.

"I see." Comprehension dawned in Will's gaze. "You're the reason she left the party so quickly last night. Last I knew, she'd gone out on the terrace for some air, and the next, she'd begged off with a headache."

"I'm sorry," James said earnestly. "I didn't plan for any of this to happen. But Bella deserves better than to be thought of as currency. She's funny and incredible and—"

He broke off before he said something he couldn't take back, like *she's the hottest kisser I've ever met*. Somehow, he didn't think that would go over well.

"You've got it bad." Will didn't bother to hide his smirk. "Never would have thought I'd see the day. She's really got you wrapped, doesn't she?"

As if Bella called the shots or something? James tried to do the right thing one time and all he got was grief.

"She's important," James growled. "That's all."

Will grinned mischievously, looking more like Mum than he usually did. "Ha. I wouldn't be surprised if you proposed to her before her brother's coronation."

"Propose? You mean ask her to marry me?" Ice slid down James's spine and he threw up a hand to stave off the rest of Will's outpouring of madness. "That's not what's going on here. We're just…I'm not… It's that I didn't want to poach on your territory. It's not sporting."

"Gabriella. Paulinha. Abril." Ticking them off on his fingers, Will cocked his head. "I think there was another one, but her name escapes me."

Revisionist history of the worst kind. "If I recall,

Abril went home with you. Despite the fact that I saw her first."

"But that's my point. We've competed over women in the past. But you have never come to me first." Will's phone rang, but he ignored the shrill buzz. "We've always subscribed to the may-the-best-man-win philosophy. So obviously Bella is the one."

Yeah, the one James wanted in his bed. That was it. Once they burned off the blinding attraction, they'd part amicably. "No way. You're reading into this."

An even worse thought occurred to him then. Did *Bella* think there was more going on here? Like maybe James wanted to take Will's place in the diabolical bridal bargain their fathers had struck? Surely not. There'd been plenty of flirting, and lots of use of the word *naked*. But no one had said anything about being serious.

Will shook his head, a smile still tugging at his lips. "I don't think so. Put your money where your mouth is."

"A bet? Seriously?" All the long hours in the service of Patrick Rowling's ego had obviously pickled his brother's brain.

"As a heart attack." Nodding at James's wrist, he pursed his lips for a beat. "Grandfather's watch. That's how bad I think you've got it. If you propose to Bella before Gabriel Montoro takes the throne, you give it to me, free and clear."

James laughed. "You are so on."

What a stupid thing to ask for. Will knew how much James loved his grandfather's watch. It was one of the few mementos from England that James had left, and Grandfather had given it to him on his eighteenth birthday. Losing it was not happening. Proposing to Bella was not happening, before the coronation or after.

Sucker's bet. James rubbed his hands together gleefully. "If I don't propose, then what? Make this worth my while."

"I'll come up with something."

James and Will shook on it.

"So this means the arranged marriage is totally off, right?" No point in going through all of this just to find out Will was toying with him.

"Totally off."

A glint in his brother's eye caught his crossways. "You were never interested in her."

"Never," Will confirmed solemnly. "Bella's got

all the right parts and everything, and she would have opened up some interesting possibilities for Rowling. But she's not my type. I'm fine with cancelling the whole agreement."

Not his type. That was insane. How could Bella not be every red-blooded man's type? "You'll talk to Father?"

"Sure. It's better coming from me anyway. Now get out so I can run this company."

James got out. He had a naked princess in his future after all.

Bella's eyes started to ache after thirty minutes of trying to read the tiny map print.

"I give up," she muttered and switched off the lamp adorning her bedside table.

All of the words were in Spanish anyway. How was she supposed to use this map Alex Ramon's assistant had given her to find the farmhouse Tía Isabella had mentioned?

When Bella had asked Rafael about it, he sent her to speak with Alex Ramon, Alma's deputy prime minister of commerce. His assistant helped her scour the royal archives until they found one solitary mention of the abandoned farmhouse in a long list of Montoro holdings. But there was little to go on location-wise other than *Aldeia Dormer*, the name of a tiny village.

At least Mr. Ramon's assistant had managed to find the key to the property tucked away in a filing cabinet, a real plus. Assuming the key still worked, that was.

Now she just had to find the farmhouse. Tía Isabella's urgency had taken root, not to mention a healthy dose of curiosity about how an old farmhouse counted as part of a legacy. There was no way Bella would actually give up.

Plus, finding the farmhouse was a project, her gift to Isabella. Bella needed a local with plenty of time on his hands and access to a vehicle to help her scour the countryside for this farmhouse. And who didn't mind ditching her babysitters-slash-security guys.

Her phone rang. She glanced at it and frowned at the unfamiliar number. That was the second time today and the first caller had been Will. Dare she hope this might be the brother she'd rather talk to? "Hello?"

"You haven't been to the beach all day." James's smooth voice slid through her like silk.

"Was I supposed to be at the beach?" With a wide grin, she flipped over on her back to stare at the ceiling above her bed, completely uninterested in cryptic maps now that she had a much better distraction.

"How else am I supposed to run into you?" he pointed out. "You never gave me your phone number."

Because he'd never asked. "Yet it appears I'm speaking to you on the phone at this very minute."

"A bloke has to be resourceful around this island if he wants to ask a princess out on a date. Apparently."

A little thrill burst through her midsection. After walking away from James at the party, she'd mentally prepared for any eventuality. A woman didn't get between brothers, and James, for all his squawking about being a bad boy, wouldn't have pursued her if Will had called dibs.

And then there was always the possibility James would grow weary of all the obstacles between them. She didn't have any guarantees she'd even hear from him again.

"This is your idea of resourceful? What did you do, hit up Will for my phone number?"

James cleared his throat. "I talked to him. About us."

That was pretty much an admission of how he'd gotten her number. "Yeah. He told me."

"Well, half my battle is won. My day will be complete if you would kindly get your gorgeous rear down to the beach."

Scrambling from the bed, Bella tore off her shorts as she dashed for the dresser and wedged the phone under her chin to pull out a bikini. "What if I'm busy?"

"Cancel. In fact, cancel everything for the rest of the day."

The rest of the day with James? She was so on board with that plan, she could hardly keep the giddiness in check. But she couldn't let *him* know how much she was into him. That was rule number one.

"You'll have to give me more than that in order for me to clear my schedule." She whipped her shirt off one-handed, knocking the phone to the floor. She cursed and dove for it. "I'm American. We invented high-maintenance dating. Make it worth my while."

Head tight to her shoulder so the phone didn't

try another escape attempt, she wiggled out of her underwear.

"Trust me, sweetheart," he said with a chuckle. "I've been all over the world. I'm more than capable of handling one tiny American. If you want to find out how worth it I am, walk out the door."

"I'm not dressed," she informed him saucily. Even someone as fashion savvy as Bella couldn't tie a bikini with one hand. And for some reason, now that he knew she was naked, it was an oddly effective turn-on.

"Perfect," he purred. "I like a woman who can read my mind. What am I thinking right now?"

If it was anything close to what she was thinking, a public beach was not the best place for them to be together. "You're thinking that you'd better hang up so I can, you know, leave the house."

His laugh rolled through her and then cut off abruptly as the call ended. She hummed as she threw on her bikini and covered it with a short dress made of fishnet weave.

She hit the foyer in under three minutes and almost escaped without her security detail noticing her stealthy exit, when she heard the voice of doom call out behind her.

"Isabella."

Groaning, she turned to face her father since the cover up was just as see-through from the front as the back. The faster she withdrew from his clutches, the better. "Yeah, Dad."

"I understand you told Will Rowling you weren't interested in him. I'm very disappointed."

Of course he was. He'd have to smooth things over with Patrick Rowling and figure out another way to make everyone miserable.

"That's me. The disappointing daughter," she admitted lightly, hoping if she kept her cool, the extraction might go faster. She had a man waiting patiently for her on the beach.

"You cannot continue behaving this way. Marriage to Rowling will settle you and nothing else seems to work to that end. You must repair your relationship with him."

His hand flew up to staunch the protest she'd been about to voice.

"No, Isabella. This is a serious matter, among other serious matters I must discuss with you. However, I'm expected to accompany Gabriel to a royal function. Be here when I get back," her father commanded.

"Sure, Dad." She fled before he could tell her when he'd be back because then she could claim ignorance when she wasn't here.

Her stomach tightened as she walked down the narrow cliffside stairs to the beach. Why couldn't she have timed that better? The encounter put a damper on the joy she'd had since the moment she'd heard James's voice.

When her toes sank into the sand, she scoured the sun-worshippers for a glimpse of the whipcord physique she couldn't erase from her mind. James was easy to spot in a turquoise shirt that shielded his British complexion from the rays. Sunglasses covered his beautiful eyes and as always, he wore the expensive watch he never seemed to leave home without. He lay stretched out on a towel off to the side of the crowd, lounging in his own little cleared area.

"Thought you'd never get here," he commented when she flopped down next to him. He paused and whipped off his glasses to focus on her intently. "What's wrong?"

How bad was it that he made her so mushy just by noticing that she was a little upset? "Nothing. My father."

"Say no more." James shook his head and sat up to clasp her hand in his, squeezing it once. "I've been avoiding mine since the pictures hit."

"What pictures?"

"You don't know?" When she shook her head, he rubbed his face with his free hand. "Someone snapped us with me on top of you when you tripped over my chair the other day. We were on the front page of the Playa Del Sol newspaper. And probably all the other ones, too. I'm sorry, I figured you'd seen them. Or had a confrontation with your father about them."

Oh, that explained a lot, especially Rafael's use of his boardroom voice. "I learned the hard way to never search my name on the internet, so no, I haven't seen the pictures. And I think I just narrowly missed that confrontation. The one I had was bad enough, but fortunately, he was too busy to give me a proper talking to. I'm supposed to be home when he gets back so I can obediently listen to his lecture. Oops."

James flashed a quick grin. "You're my kind of woman."

"We seem to have a flagrant disregard for authority in common, don't we?"

"When it makes sense," James corrected. "You're not sixteen. You're a grown woman who can make her own choices. If you want to be with me, you should get that opportunity, authority figures aside."

As much as she liked his point, she was still a member of the royal family and the idea of smarmy pictures floating around upset her, especially when the actual event had been so innocuous.

"So we're both rebels, but only when presented with pigheaded fathers?"

"Exactly." His thumb smoothed over hers and he had yet to return his sunglasses to their perch over his eyes. The way he was looking at her, as if he understood her so perfectly, they didn't even need words—it took a massive amount of willpower to not throw herself into his arms.

Why were they outside in plain sight again? Her babysitters could lumber down the stairs from the house at any moment, squelching what promised to be an adventurous day.

"This wasn't exactly what I had in mind for our first date," she remarked with an exaggerated glance around. "Too many people and I'm pretty sure I remember something about getting naked.

I readily admit to bucking authority when called for, but I am not a fan of sand in certain places. What shall we do about that?"

James's blue eyes went sultry and he gripped her hand tighter. "A little bird told me you were high maintenance, so I was going to take you to dinner later at Casa Branca in Del Sol. But I see the huge gaping flaw in that plan since you would indeed have to be dressed for that."

"It's also pretty public. I'd love to escape prying eyes, security details and cameras for at least one night." She frowned. Was nowhere sacred enough to spend time with a man she was just getting to know without fear of creating a whole brand-new scandal? "Can we go back to your place?"

They certainly couldn't go to hers, not with the royal lecture pending.

"Ha." James rolled his eyes, turning them a myriad of blues in the sunlight. "I can only imagine dear old Dad's aneurism when I walk through the front door with you."

No, neither of them were sixteen but it felt that way when they couldn't even find a place to be alone without overbearing parents around. So it was time for an adult solution.

"New plan," Bella chirped. "I've heard a rumor of an abandoned farmhouse that's part of our family's royal property. But I don't know where it is. I need someone with a car and a good knowledge of the roads in Alma to help me find it. Know anyone like that who's also free to drive around with me?"

"James's Abandoned Farmhouse Locators, at your service." He bowed over her hand with mock ceremony. "Let's plan on making a night of it. We'll get some takeout. Do you want to run back upstairs to grab a few things?"

"Give me five minutes." She mentally packed an overnight bag. Had she brought that smoking hot lingerie set she hadn't worn yet?

"Four." He raised her hand to his lips and kissed it. "That bikini is killing me. I want to untie it with my teeth and take a good hard look at what's underneath. Then my mouth will be busy getting acquainted with every inch of your naked body."

She shuddered as his words lanced through her core with a long tug. "I'll be back in three."

Six

The small cockpit of James's car filled with the scent of Bella instantly. It was exotic, erotic and engaging, flipping switches in his body he'd have sworn were already wide open from the visual of Bella at the beach in that little bikini.

How was it possible to be even more turned on when you were already blind from lack of release?

She'd changed into a little white sundress that hugged her curves. The tiny straps begged for a man's hands to slip them off her shoulders, kiss the smooth flesh and then keep going into the deep V of her cleavage.

It was going to be a long, long drive through the interior of Alma as they looked for an abandoned farmhouse Bella insisted they could find. Problem was, he wanted her now, not in two hours after they crisscrossed the island in his green Lamborghini, which was hardly invisible.

As they clicked their seatbelts, his phone buzzed and he glanced at it out of habit, already planning to ignore whatever it was. Nothing could be more important than Bella.

Except it was a text message from Will. Who never texted him. Frowning, James tapped the screen of his phone and read the message.

I had nothing to do with this, but thought you should know.

Nothing good was going to come of clicking the link Will had sent, but forewarned was forearmed, so James did it anyway.

Montoro Princess to Wed the Heir to Rowling Energy.

The headline was enough. He didn't need to read the rest.

With a curse, he tilted his phone toward Bella. "Now taking bets on which of our fathers is behind this."

She glanced at it and repeated his curse, but substituted the vilest word with a more ladylike version, which put a smile on his face despite the ill-timed, fabricated announcement.

"Mine," she announced with a snort. "Control and dictate is exactly his style."

"Sure you're not describing my father?" James returned. "Because that's his MO all day long."

"No, it's my father. Definitely. But it doesn't matter." She grabbed his phone, switched it off and stuffed it in the bag at her feet. "You can't have that back. No more scandals, interfering fathers and marriage alliances. Just drive." She glanced over her shoulder. "And now. Before my babysitters figure out I'm not in the house."

Since that sounded fine to him, he backed out of his beachside parking place and floored the gas pedal, heading west out of Playa Del Onda.

"This is a gorgeous car," she commented with apparent appreciation as she caressed the dashboard lovingly in a way that immediately made him want her hand in his lap instead of on his car. "I dated a guy in Miami with an Aventador, but it's so flashy without any real substance. The Gallardo is more refined and I love the color."

God, she *was* going to kill him before the day

was over. "You know cars? I can't begin to tell you how hot that is."

She shrugged with a musical laugh, knocking one of the straps of her dress askew and drawing his attention away from the road. Dangerously.

"It's hard to live in a place like Miami without gaining at least some passing knowledge. I'll let you in on a secret, though. We girls always judge a man by his car. Mercedes-Benz? Too serious. Porsche? Works too hard. Corvette? Too worried about his hair."

James laughed in spite of the discomfort going on down below that likely wouldn't ease for an eternity. "So my Lamborghini is the only reason you wanted to go out with me?"

"The car test only works if you haven't met the guy yet. We're strictly talking about taking someone's measure in the parking lot."

He shifted to take a hairpin curve as they wound away from the beach into the more sparsely populated inland roads of Alma. Since he had no idea what they were looking for, he'd drive and let her do the surveying.

"Then I'll go with my second guess. You wanted to go out with me because I'm a witty conversationalist." He waggled his brows and shot her a sly smile. "Or door number three—I know a trick or two between the sheets."

He'd meant to be flirtatious, but now that it was out there, he realized the conversation with Will still bothered him a bit. Bella had said on numerous occasions that marriage wasn't her thing. Regardless, establishing the ground rules of what they were doing here couldn't hurt.

"Both." Blond hair swinging, she leaned on the emergency brake between them, so close he imagined he could hear her heart beating. "We have all night long and I do love a good conversation, especially in the dark. But if you forced me to choose, I'd go with door number three."

Brilliant. So they were both on the same page. They were hot for each other and wanted to burn it off with a wild night together. "Just so you know, with me, sheets are optional."

Awareness tightened the atmosphere as she let her gaze travel down his chest and rest on the bulge in his pants. He could hardly keep his attention on the road. Who wanted to watch the scraggly countryside of Alma when a goddess sat in the adjacent seat?

"By the way," she said. "I think we just passed the road we were supposed to take."

With a groan, he did a quick U-turn and drove down the street barely noticeable in the overgrowth of trees and groundcover. "I didn't know we had directions. Maybe you could speak up earlier next time?"

"Sorry, I'm a little distracted. Maybe you could stop being so sexy for a couple of minutes." Fanning herself as if he'd heated her up, she trailed a finger down his bicep muscle and toyed with the crook of his elbow.

"Me?" he growled. "You're the one in that knockout dress. All I can hear in my head is your voice on repeat, when you said the next time we were together, you'd be naked."

"Oh, did I forget to tell you?" She kissed the tip of her finger and pressed it to his lips, but she pulled away too quickly for him to suck the finger into his mouth the way he wanted to. "I'm naked under this dress. Wanna pull over?"

He nearly whimpered. "I cannot possibly explain how much I would like to do exactly that. But we are not getting it on in the car like a couple of horny teenagers. You deserve to be treated right and that includes a bed and me taking my time enjoying you."

Besides, they might be headed into the heart of rural Alma, but the roads were not deserted. They passed cars constantly. People knew who drove the only green Lamborghini on the island and all it would take was one idiot with a camera phone for another risqué picture of James and Bella together to land in the public eye. It was a dirty shame he hadn't tinted the windows on his car.

Until they straightened out the marriage announcement, it would create so much less of a jumble if they kept a low profile.

"Then drive faster," Bella suggested, and her hand wandered over to rest on his inner thigh, where she casually stroked him. Innocently, as if she touched him all the time, except she hadn't touched him like *that* before and his vision started to blur with unrequited lust.

He stepped on the gas. Hard.

"Where are we going?" Driving around until they stumbled over a farmhouse that may or may not exist had started to sound like the worst idea he'd ever agreed to.

"This is the main road to Aldeia Dormer, right?"

When he nodded, she pointed at the horizon. "The assistant I talked to thought she remembered that the farmhouse was on the outskirts, before you hit the village. If you keep going, we'll find out."

"What if I just take you to a hotel and we check in under an assumed name?"

He had plenty of practice with parking in an obscure place and passing out discrete tips to the staff so he and his lady friend could duck through the kitchen entrance. Why hadn't he insisted on that in the first place? The text from Will had muddled him up, obviously. There was a former castillo-turned-four-star-bed-and-breakfast on the south side of Playa Del Onda that he wouldn't mind trying.

She shook her head with a sad smile and it was so much the opposite of her normal sunny demeanor, he immediately wanted to say something to lighten the mood. But what had caused such an instant mood shift?

"My aunt asked me to find the farmhouse. It's important to her and maybe to Gabriel. She said it was part of the Montoro legacy. We're already so close. I promise, if we don't find it soon, I'll reconsider the hotel."

Her earnestness dug under his skin and there was no way he could refuse. "Sure. We'll keep going."

Okay, maybe she was a little different from other women he'd dated. He certainly couldn't recall catering to one so readily before, but that was probably due to the degree of difficulty he'd experienced in getting this one undressed and under him.

They drove for a couple of miles, wrapped in tension. Just when James started to curse his flamboyant taste in cars, they crested a hill, and she gasped as a white farmhouse came into view.

Wonders of wonders. "Is that it?"

"I'm not sure." Bella pursed her lips as he drove off the main road onto the winding path to the farmhouse and parked under a dangerously dilapidated carport.

Would serve him right if this ill-conceived jaunt through Alma resulted in a hundred grand worth of bodywork repairs when the carport collapsed on the Lamborghini. "I thought you said it was off this road."

"Well, it's supposed to be. But I've never been here before," she pointed out. "Maybe there are a hundred white farmhouses between here and Aldeia Dormer."

"Only one way to find out." He helped her from the car and held her hand as they picked through the overgrown property. "Don't step in the tall weed patches. There might be something living in them you'd rather not tangle with."

She squeezed his hand. "I'm glad you're here, then. I'll let you deal with the creepy crawly stuff."

"I'll be your hero any day."

Her grateful smile made his chest tight with a foreign weight because he felt like a fraud all at once. The only heroic thing he'd ever done in his life was give Bella an opportunity to be with Will if she chose. When had he last expended any appreciable effort looking out for someone else's welfare?

He could start right now, if he wanted to. No reason he couldn't keep an eye out for opportunities to throw himself in front of a bullet—figuratively speaking—for an amazing woman like Bella. If she'd smile at him like that again, the payoff wasn't too shabby.

The farmhouse's original grandeur still shone through despite the years of neglect. Once, the two-story clapboard house had likely been the home of a large family, where they gathered around an old wooden table at supper to laugh and tell stories as dogs ran underfoot.

As if he knew anything about what a family did at supper. Especially a family whose members liked each other and spent time together on purpose. Did that kind of lovely fairy tale even exist outside of movies? He swallowed the stupid lump in his throat. Who cared? He had no roots and liked it that way.

The property spread beyond the house into a small valley. Chickens had probably clucked in the wide backyard, scolding fat pigs or horses that lived in the wooden pens just barely visible from the front of the house. The fences had long fallen to the weed-choked ground, succumbing to weathering and decay.

James nearly tripped over an equally weathered rectangular wooden board hidden by the grass and weeds. He kicked at it, but it was solid enough not to move much despite the force of his well-toned football muscles. Metal loops across the top caught his attention and he leaned down to ease the board up on its side.

"It's a sign," Bella whispered as her gaze lit on the opposite side.

James spun around to view the front. In bold, blocky letters, the sign read *Escondite Real*. "In more ways than one."

Unless he missed his guess, this was indeed the property of royalty. Or someone's idea of a joke.

"No one told me to brush up on my Spanish before I came here. What does it say?" Bella asked with a mock pout.

"Royal Hideaway. Is this where your ancestors came to indulge in illicit affairs?"

Mischievously, she winked at James. "If not, it's where the current generation will."

"Illicit affairs are my favorite." Taking her hand again, he guided her toward the house.

"Look. It's beautiful."

Bella pointed at a butterfly the size of his palm. It alighted on a purple bougainvillea that had thrived despite the lack of human attention, the butterfly's wings touching and separating slowly. But the sight couldn't keep his attention, not when Bella's face had taken on a glow in the late afternoon sunlight as she smiled at the butterfly.

God, she was the most exquisite woman he'd ever seen. And that was saying something when he'd been hit on by women renowned the world over for their beauty.

"Let's check out the inside." He cleared the catch from his throat, mystified by where it had come from. Women were a dime a dozen. Why didn't Bella seem like one of the legion he could have in his bed tomorrow?

It didn't matter. Will hadn't seen what he thought he'd seen when James cleared the air with him. The watch on his wrist wasn't going anywhere anytime soon.

Bella fished a set of keys from her bag. The second one turned the tumblers in the padlock on the splintered front door. It opened easily but the interior was dark and musty. Of course. There wouldn't be any electricity at an abandoned farmhouse. Or a cleaning crew.

"I guess we should have thought this through a little better," James said. "At least we know we're in the right place since the key worked."

Any hope of stripping Bella out of that little dress and spending the night in a haze of sensual pleasure vanished as something that sounded as if it had more feet than a football team scrabbled across the room.

"Yeah. It's a little more rustic than I was anticipating." She scowled at the gloom. "I'm not well versed in the art of abandoned farmhouses. Now what?"

Bella bit her lip to staunch the flow of frustrated tears. Which didn't exactly work.

This was all her fault. She'd envisioned a romantic rendezvous with a sexy, exciting man—one she'd looked forward to getting to know *very* well—and never once had it crossed her mind that "abandoned" didn't mean that someone had picked up and left a fully functioning house, ready and waiting for her and James to borrow for a night or two. The most strenuous thing she'd expected to do before letting James seduce her was kill a spider in the shower.

Graying sheets covered in cobwebs and dust obscured what she assumed must be furnishings underneath. The farmhouse hadn't been lived in for a long time. Decades maybe. The property may not even have running water. She shuddered. What had Isabella sent her into?

One tear shook loose and slid down her face.

Without speaking, James took her hand and drew

her into his embrace, which immediately calmed her. How had he known that was what she needed? She slid her arms around his waist and laid her head on his strong chest.

Goodness. His athlete's physique did it for her in so many ways. He was shockingly solid and muscular for someone so lean and her own body woke up in a hurry. Sensation flooded her and she ached for him to kiss her again, as he'd done on the terrace—hot, commanding and so very sexy.

But then he drew back and tipped her chin up, his gaze serious and a bit endearing. "Here's what we're going to do. I'll drive into the village and pick up a few things. I hate to leave you here, but we can't be photographed together. While I'm gone, see if you can find a way to clean up at least one room."

His smile warmed her and she returned it, encouraged by his optimism. "You do have a gift for uncomplicating things. I'm a little jealous," she teased.

"It'll be smashing. I promise."

He left and she turned her attention to the great room of the farmhouse. Once she pulled the drapes aside, sunlight shafted into the room through the wide windows, catching on the dusty chandelier. So the house was wired for electricity. That was a plus. Maybe she could figure out how to get it activated—for next time, obviously, because there was a distinct possibility she and James might make long-term use out of this hideaway. Being a princess had to be worth something, didn't it?

Holding her breath, she pulled the sheets from the furnishings, raising a tornado of dust that made her sneeze. Once all the sheets were in a pile in the corner, she dashed from the room to give all the flurries a chance to settle. Using her phone as a flashlight, she found a broom in one of the closets of the old-fashioned kitchen.

"Cinderella, at your service," she muttered and carried the broom like a sword in front of her in case she ran into something crawly since her knight had left.

By the time he returned, the sun had started to set. She'd swept the majority of the dust from the room and whacked the cobwebs from the corners and chandelier. The throaty growl of the Lamborghini echoed through the great room as James came up the drive and parked. The car door slammed and James appeared in the open door-way, his arms weighted down with bags.

"Wow." He whistled. "This place was something back in the day, huh?"

She glanced around at the rich furnishings, which were clearly high-end, even for antiques, and still quite functional if you didn't mind the grime. "It's a property owned by royalty. I guess they didn't spare much expense, regardless of the location. I wonder why no one has been here for so long?"

And why all these lovely antiques were still here, like ghosts frozen in time until someone broke the spell.

"Tantaberra liked Del Sol." James set his bags down carefully on the coffee table and began pulling out his bounty. "My guess is this was too far out of the limelight and too pedestrian for his taste."

A variety of candles appeared from the depths of the first bag. James scouted around until he found an empty three-pronged candelabra, screwed tapers into it and then flicked a lighter with his other hand. He shut the front door, plunging the room into full darkness. The soft glow of the candles bathed his face in mellow light and she forgot all about the mystery of this farmhouse as he set the candelabra on the mantel behind the brocade couch.

"Nice. What else did you bring me?" Bella asked, intrigued at the sheer number of bags James had returned with. She'd expected dinner and that was about it.

"The most important thing." He yanked a plaid blanket from the second bag and spread it out on the floor. "Can't have you dining on these rough plank floors, now can we?"

She shook her head with a smile and knelt down on the soft blanket to watch him continue unpacking. It seemed as if he'd thought of everything, down to such necessary but unique details as a blanket and candles. It was a quality she would never have thought to admire or even notice. And in James, it was potently attractive.

"Second most important—wine." He plunked the bottle next to her and pulled out two plastic cups. "Not the finest stemware. Sorry. It was the best I could do."

His chagrin was heartbreakingly honest. Did he

think she'd turn up her nose at his offering? Well, some women probably would, but not Bella.

"It's perfect," she said sincerely. "If you'll give me the corkscrew, I'll pour while you show me what else you found in town."

He handed her a small black-cased device of some sort. It looked like a pocketknife and she eyed it curiously until he flicked out the corkscrew with a half laugh. "Never seen one of these before?"

"My wine is typically poured for me," she informed him pertly with a mock haughty sneer, lady-of-the-manor style. "Cut me some slack."

Instead of grinning back, he dropped to the blanket and took her hand. "This is a crappy first date. I wish I could have taken you to dinner in Del Sol, like I'd planned. You deserve to be waited on hand and foot and for me to make love to you on silk sheets. I'm sorry that things are so out of control for us right now. I'll make it up to you, I swear."

"Oh, James." Stricken, she stared into his gorgeous aqua eyes flickering in the candlelight. "This is exactly what I've been envisioning since I got in the car back at the beach. I don't need a three-hundred-euro dinner. I just want to be with you."

"You're a princess," he insisted fiercely. "I want to treat you like the royalty you are."

Good grief. Was all this because of the stupid joke she'd made about being high maintenance? Obviously he'd taken her at her word. Backpedaling time.

"You do that every time we're together. Encouraging me to make my own choices about who I date. Bringing me to the farmhouse simply because I asked, without telling me it was crazy. Holding me when I cry. Being my hero by making this night romantic with ingenuity and flair, despite the less than stellar accommodations. How could I possibly find fault in any of that?"

A little overcome, she stared at him, hoping to impart her sincerity by osmosis. Because he was amazing and somehow verbalizing it made it more real. Who else in her life had ever done such wonderful things for her? No one. Tender, fledgling feelings for James welled up and nearly splashed over.

He scowled. "I did those things because you needed me to. Not because you're a princess."

Silly man. He didn't get what she was saying at all. "But don't you see? I need someone to treat me like *me*. Because you *see* me and aren't wrapped up in all the royal trappings, which are essentially meaningless at the end of the day."

That was the mistake her father had made, trying to pawn her off on Will. And Will was nearly as bad. Everyone was far more impressed with her royal pedigree than she ever was. Everyone except James. And now he was being all weird about it.

Just as fiercely, she gripped his hand. "I wasn't a princess last year and if you'd met me then, wouldn't you have tried to give me what I needed instead of trying to cater to some idea you have about how a girl with royal blood should expect you to act?"

"Yeah." He blew out a breath. "I would. I just didn't want this to be so disappointing for you. Not our first time together."

Seriously? After the way he'd kissed her on the terrace? There was no freaking way he'd disappoint her, whether it was their first time or hundredth time. The location hardly mattered. She wanted the man, not some luxury vacation. If he thought dollar signs turned her on, she'd done something wrong.

"Our first time together cannot be disappointing, because you're half the equation," she chided gently. "I expect fireworks simply because you're the one setting them off. Okay?"

He searched her expression, brows drawn together. "If you're sure."

She caressed his arm soothingly, hoping to loosen him up a little. The romantic candlelit atmosphere was going to waste and that was a shame. "Yeah. Now show me what else is in your magic bag."

With a grin, he grabbed the last bag. He fished out a roll of salami, which he set by the wine, then lined up a wedge of cheese, boxed crackers and a string of grapes. "Dinner. I wish it—"

"Stop. It's food and I'm hungry. Sit down and let's eat it while you tell me stories about growing up in Alma." Patting the blanket, she concentrated on opening the wine, her one self-appointed task in the evening's preparations. It was tougher to pierce the cork than she'd anticipated.

Instead of complying with her suggestion, he took the bottle from her hands and expertly popped the cork in under fifteen seconds.

"You've done that before," she accused with a laugh as he poured two very full glasses of the chilled white wine. It was pretty good for a no-name label and she swallowed a healthy bit.

"Yep. I'm a master of all things decadent." He arched a brow and plucked a grape from the bunch to run it across her lips with slow sensuality that fanned heat across her skin instantly. "Hurry up and eat so I can show you."

Watching him with unabashed invitation, she let him ease the grape between her lips and accepted it with a swirl of her tongue across the tips of his fingers. His eyelids lowered, fluttering slightly, and he deliberately set his glass of wine on the coffee table, as if to silently announce he planned to use both hands in very short order.

She shuddered as all the newly-awakened feelings for this man twined with the already-powerful attraction. She wanted to explore his depths and let the amazing things happening between them explode. Simple desire she understood and appreciated, but this went beyond anything simple, beyond anything she'd experienced before.

"Or we can do both at the same time," she suggested, her voice dropping huskily as he trailed his wet fingertip down her chin and throat to trace the line of her cleavage.

"There you go again reading my mind," he murmured and captured another grape without looking away, his gaze hot and full of promise. "Let's see if you can guess what I'm thinking now."

Seven

James outlined Bella's full lips with the grape and then ran it down her throat, resting it in the hollow of her collarbone. Slowly, he leaned over and drew the fruit into his mouth, sucking at her fragrant skin as he crushed the grape in his teeth simultaneously.

The combination of Bella and sweet juice sang across his taste buds. She was exquisitely, perfectly made and he wanted her with an unparalleled passion that wiped his mind of everything else.

Flinging her head back to give him better access, she gulped in a breath and exhaled on a low moan that tightened his whole body.

"Instead of reading your mind," she said, her low

voice burrowing into his abdomen, spreading heat haphazardly, "why don't you surprise me with a few more strategically placed grapes?"

"You like that?"

Grapes as a seduction method—that was a first. And now he was wishing he'd bought a bushel. Gripping another one, he traced it between her breasts and circled one of her nipples. It peaked beautifully under the filmy sundress.

How had he gotten so supremely lucky as to have such a beautiful, exciting woman within arm's reach? One who didn't require him to rain expensive gifts down on her, but seemed perfectly content with simple trappings and a man paying attention to her.

All the talk of heroics made his skin crawl. She was sorely mistaken if she thought of him as a hero, but the look in her eyes—well, that made him feel ten feet tall, as if he could do anything as long as she believed in him.

The power of it emboldened him.

Urgently, he lunged for her, catching her up in his arms as he laid her back on the blanket. Her lips crashed against his in a hot, wet kiss that went on and on as their tongues explored and dipped and mated. Her body twined with his and finally, she was underneath him, his thigh flush against her core. Her hands went on a mission to discover every part of his back and he reveled in the feminine touch he'd been craving for so long.

Hooking the neckline of her dress, he dragged it from her breast. As her flesh was revealed, he followed the trail with his mouth, nibbling and kissing until his lips closed over her nipple.

She arched against his mouth, pushing herself deeper inside as he reached for a handful of grapes. With little regard for decorum, he lifted his head and crushed the fruit savagely, letting the juice drip onto her peaked nipple. The liquid wetted the tip as she watched with dark eyes; her glistening breast was so erotic, he groaned even as he leaned forward to catch an errant drop on his tongue.

Licking upward until he hit her nipple again, he sucked all the juice off to the sound of her very vocal sighs of pleasure. That nearly undid him.

"I want to see all of you," he murmured and his need was so great, he didn't even wait for her reply. Peeling off that little dress counted as one of the greatest pleasures of his life as inch by inch, he uncovered her incredible skin.

"You're so beautiful," he told her with a catch in his throat.

Something unnamable had overcome him. Something dramatic and huge. But he liked it and before whatever it was fled, he pulled a string of condoms from his pocket and rolled to the side to shed his own clothes so he could feel every gorgeous bit of her against him.

When he was naked, he rolled back, intending to gather up that bundle of heaven back into his arms, but she stopped him with a palm to his chest. "Not yet. I want to see you, too."

Her gaze roved over his body and lingered in unexpected places. His thighs. His pectorals. Her palm spread and flattened over his nipple, as if she wanted to grab hold.

When she couldn't, she purred. "Hard as stone. I like that."

"I like you touching me."

"Allow me to continue." Wicked smile spreading across her face, she ran both hands down the planes of his chest and onto his thighs, right past the area he'd hoped she was headed for. Which of course made him anticipate the return journey.

Her fingernails scraped his leg muscles lightly,

and she trailed one hand over his hip to explore his butt, which tightened automatically under the onslaught. *Everything* tightened with unanswered release, including the parts he'd have sworn were already stretched to the point of bursting.

He groaned as heat exploded under her hands. His hips strained toward her, muscles begging to be set free from the iron hold he had on them. "Are you trying to make me barmy?"

"Nope. Just looking for the best places for when it's my turn with the grapes."

"Oh, it's totally your turn," he countered. "This is your dinner, too, and you must be hungry."

"At last." She knelt, grabbed a grape and eyed his splayed body. "Hmm. Where to start? I know."

She stuck the grape in her mouth and rolled it around with her tongue, her hot gaze on his erection. Somehow that was more arousing than if she'd actually tongued *him*. She caught the small globe in her front teeth and bent to run it over his torso, dipping into the valleys and peaks, her hair spreading out like a feathery torture device across his sensitive skin. When she accidentally—or maybe on purpose—dragged her hair over his erection, the light touch lit him up. Fire radiated from the juncture of his thighs outward and just as he was about to cup her head to guide her toward the prize, she leaned up on her haunches.

Plucking the grape from between her lips, she grazed his length with the wet grape, nearly causing him to spill everything in one pulse.

"Enough of that," he growled, manacling her wrist to draw it away from the line of fire. "You've obviously underestimated my appetite. Time for the main course."

She grinned. "I thought you'd never say that."

Fumbling with a condom, he somehow managed to get it secured and then rolled her underneath him. He'd been fantasizing about taking her exactly this way for an eternity. Soft and luscious, she slid right into the curves of his body as she had that day in the sand, except this time, nothing separated their skin and it was every bit as glorious as he'd imagined.

"You—" He nearly swallowed his tongue as she shifted, rolling her hips against his. The tips of her breasts ground into his torso, and it all felt so amazing, he couldn't speak.

And then he didn't have to speak as he gazed down into her blue eyes. Candlelight danced in their depths and he caught a hint of something else that hit him in the gut. As if she'd seen pieces of him that he'd never realized were there and she liked what she'd found. As if she truly saw him as a hero. Maybe she was the only one who could relate. They were both rebels—to the rest of the world—but his pain and difficulties behind the rebellion made total sense to her.

"Bella," he murmured and that was the extent of what he could push through his tight throat.

"Right here." Her low, husky voice became his favorite part of her as it hummed through him. "I was really afraid this would never happen. Make it worth the wait."

It was already so worth it. Worth the lectures from his father, worth the uncomfortable nobleness he'd somehow adopted when around her. Worth sending her away from him on the terrace when all he'd wanted to do was pull that outrageous red dress up to her waist and make her his under the moonlight.

This way was better. Much better. No fear of being caught. No loaded landmines surrounding them, no paparazzi lying in wait to cause a scandal just because they wanted to be together.

He laid his lips on hers and fell into a long sigh of a kiss that grew urgent as she opened her mouth and dove in with her tongue, heightening the pleasure.

And then with a small shift, they joined. Easily, beautifully, as if she'd been specially crafted for James Rowling. It was almost spiritual and he'd never felt such a weight to being with a woman.

He froze for a moment, just letting her essence bleed through him, and then, determined to get her to the same place of mystical pleasure, he focused on her cries, her shifts, her rhythms. He became an instant student of Bella's pleasure until he could anticipate exactly what she wanted him to do next to drive her to release.

And then she stiffened as a volatile climax engulfed her that he felt all the way to his soles. He let go and followed her into oblivion, holding her tight because he couldn't stand to lose contact with her.

As he regained cognizance, he realized she was trying to get closer, too. He settled Bella comfortably in his arms and lay with her to watch the candle flames flicker, throwing shadows of the heavy furniture on the walls of the farmhouse they'd turned into the safest of havens.

This time with Bella...it was the most romantic experience he'd ever had, which sat strangely. For a guy who loved sex and abhorred roots, romance was difficult to come by. Not only had he never had it, he'd never sought it.

Why did something as normal as sex feel so abnormally and hugely different with this woman? He couldn't make sense of it and it bothered him. As the unsettled feeling grew, he kissed Bella's forehead and separated from her.

Bustling around to gather up their abandoned wine glasses and remnants of their dinner, he threw a forced smile over his shoulder. "Ready to finish eating?"

She returned the smile, not seeming to realize that he was trying to mask his sudden confusion. "Depends. Is that code for round two? Because the answer is yes, if so."

Round two. He chugged some wine to give himself a second. Normally, he went for round two like a sailor on shore leave, but the thick, romantic atmosphere and the crushing sensation in his chest when he looked at Bella made him question everything.

What was going on here? This was supposed to be nothing but an opportunity to have fun with Bella, no expectations, no proposals before her brother took the throne.

"No code. Let's eat."

What was his *problem*? A beautiful woman who rocked his world wanted him to make love to her again. Maybe he should just do that, and everything would make sense once they were back to just two people having smashing sex. Will's bet had hashed everything.

"For now," he amended. "Got to keep up our strength."

She grinned and shoved some crackers in her mouth. "All done," she mumbled around the crackers.

Groaning around a laugh, he sat close to her on the blanket and shook off his strange mood. After all, she was Alma's only princess. What role did a disgraced football player have in the middle of all that? Especially when he didn't plan to be living in Alma permanently. In fact, a new contract would get him out from under all of this confusion quite well. He could enjoy a fling with Bella and jet off to another continent. Like always.

Obviously, there was no reason to give any more credence to the heavy weight in his chest.

There was a huge crick in Bella's neck, but she actually welcomed the pain. Because she'd gotten it sleeping in James's arms on a blanket spread over a hardwood floor.

That had been delicious. And wonderful. And a host of other things she could barely articulate. So she didn't, opting to see what the morning brought in this unconventional affair they'd begun.

Once they were dressed and had the curtains thrown open to let sunlight into the musty great room, she turned to James. "I don't know about you, but I'm heavily in favor of finding a café that'll give you a mountain of scrambled eggs, bacon and biscuits in a takeout box. I'm starving."

He flashed a quick grin. "Careful. That kind of comment now has all sorts of meaning attached. You better clarify whether you want me to feed you or strip you."

Laughing, she socked him on the arm. "You're

the one who started that with the grapes. And the answer to that is both. Always."

He caught her hand and held it in his. "I'm only teasing. I'll go get breakfast. I wish you could come with me. Is it too much to ask that we go on a real date where I sit with you at an actual table?"

"We'll get there." She kissed him soundly and shoved him toward the door. "Once I have food in me, we can strategize about the rest of our lives."

Item number one on the agenda: get this farmhouse in livable shape.

The strange look he shot her put a hitch in her stride and she realized immediately how he must have taken her comment. Okay, she hadn't meant it like that, as if she was assuming they'd become a dyed-in-the-wool couple and he needed to get down on one knee.

But what was so bad about making plans beyond breakfast? She'd had some great lovers in the past, but what she'd experienced with James went far beyond the category of casual. Hadn't he felt all the wonderful things she'd felt last night?

She rolled her eyes to make it harder for him to detect the swirl of emotion going on underneath the surface. "You can stop with the deer-in-the-headlights, hon. I just narrowly escaped one marriage. I'm not at all interested in jumping right into another one, no matter how good the prospective groom is at *feeding* me."

Which was absolutely, completely true. Saying it aloud solidified it for them both.

With a wicked smile, he yanked on her hand, pulling her into his embrace. His weird expression melted away as he nuzzled her neck.

Foot-in-mouth averted. Except now she was wondering exactly what his intentions toward her were. A few nights together and then ta-ta?

And when did she get to the point where that wasn't necessarily what *she* wanted? She didn't do all that commitment-and-feelings rigmarole. She liked to have fun and secretly felt sorry for women on husband-hunting missions. Her mother had gotten trapped in that cycle and lived a miserable existence for years and years as a result. *No, thank you.*

Nothing had changed just because of a few emotions she had no idea what to do with. Her affair with James had begun so unconventionally and under extreme circumstances. If they'd been able to go out on a real date from the beginning, they'd probably have already moved on by now.

Good thing she'd made it clear marriage wasn't on her mind so there was no confusion, though a few other things could be better spelled out.

James sucked on her tender flesh, clearly about to move south, and she wiggled away before her body leaped on the train without her permission.

"That wasn't supposed to be a code word." She giggled at his crestfallen expression but sobered to hold his gaze. "Listen, before you go get breakfast, let's lay this out. Last night was amazing but I'm not done. Are you? Because if this thing between us was one night only, I'll be sad, but I'm a big girl. Tell me."

He was already shaking his head before she'd finished speaking. "No way. I'm nowhere near done."

Her pulse settled. *Good answer.* "So, if you want a repeat of the grapes-on-the-floor routine, I'm all for it. But I'd prefer a real bed from now on. My plan is to put some elbow grease into this place, preferably someone else's, and create a lover's retreat where we can escape whenever we feel like it."

"Are you expecting us to have to hide out that

long?" Wary surprise crept into his tone, setting her teeth on edge.

"I don't know. Maybe." What, was it too much trouble to drive out here just to have a few stolen hours together? "Is what I'm suggesting so horrible?"

"No. Not at all. My hesitation was completely on the issue of hiding out. I want to be seen with you in public. I'm not ashamed of our relationship and I don't want you to think I am."

Her heart squished as she absorbed his righteous indignation and sincerity. He wanted their relationship to be aboveboard, just as he'd wanted to clear things with Will before proceeding. And that meant a lot to her. He kept trying to make her think he didn't have a noble bone in his body when everything he did hinged on his own personal sense of honor.

"I didn't think that, but way to score major points." She batted her eyelashes at him saucily. "But that aside, I don't even know if I'm staying in Alma permanently or I'd get my own place. I suspect you're in the same boat."

He'd told her he hoped to get another contract with a professional soccer—sorry, *football*—team, and that the team could be in Barcelona or the UK or Brazil or, or, or… He might end up anywhere in the world. And probably would.

"Yeah. I haven't made a secret out of the fact that I don't plan to stick around," he agreed cautiously.

"I know. So do you really think there's a scenario where either of us would be willing to parade the other across the thresholds of our fathers' houses even if we do clear up the engagement announcement?"

He sighed. "Yeah, you're right. Let's rewind this whole conversation. Smashing idea, Bella. I'd love to help you get this place into shape so I can take an actual shower in the morning."

That was the James she knew and loved. Or rather, the James she…didn't know very well, but liked a whole lot. With a sigh, she let him kiss her again and shoved him out the door for real this time because her stomach was growling and her heart was doing some funny things that she didn't especially like.

Space would be good right now.

The sound of the Lamborghini's engine faded away as she went about taking inventory on the lower floor. Apparently most, if not all, of the original furnishings remained, as evidenced by their arrangement. Bella had been in enough wealthy households to recognize when a place had been artfully decorated and this one definitely had. The pieces had been placed just so by a feminine hand, or at least she imagined it that way. That's when it hit her that this farmhouse had probably once belonged to an ancestor of hers. Someone of her blood.

A long gone Montoro, forgotten for ages once the coup deposed the royal family. She'd never felt very connected to the monarchy, not even at the palace in Del Sol where some of the original riches of the royal estate were housed. But the quieter treasures of the farmhouse struck her differently.

She picked up a filthy urn resting on a side table. White, or at least it was under the grime. She rubbed at it ineffectually with her palm and managed to get a small bit of the white showing. The eggshell-like surface was pretty.

Maybe it wasn't priceless like the Qing Dynasty porcelain vase sitting in an art niche at the Coral Gables house. But worth something. Maybe it was actually worth more than the million-dollar piece of pottery back in Miami because it had been used by someone.

She'd never thought about worth being tied to something's usefulness. But she liked the idea of having a purpose. She'd had one in Miami—wildlife conservation. What had happened to that passion? It was as if she'd come to Alma and forgotten how great it made her feel to do something worthwhile.

With renewed fervor, she dove into cleaning what she could with the meager supplies at hand, and revised her earlier thoughts. It would be fun to put some elbow grease of her own into this house. Whom else could she trust with her family's property?

When the purr of James's car finally reverberated through the open door, she glanced at her dirty arms and her lip curled. Some princess she looked like. A Cinderella in reverse—she'd gone from the royal palace to being a slave to the dust. A shower sounded like heaven about now.

The look in James's eye when he walked in holding a bag stenciled with the logo of the only chain restaurant in Alma had her laughing. "There is no way you're thinking what I think you're thinking. I'm filthy."

"Yes, way." He hummed in approval. "I've never

seen a sexier woman than you, Bella Montoro. Layer of dirt or not."

There he went again making her insides all melty and that much more raw. She always got the distinct feeling he saw the real her, past all the outside stuff and into her core. The outside, inconsequential stuff was invisible to him. Coupled with the hard twist of pure lust she got pretty much any time she laid eyes on him, she could hardly think around it.

She shook it off. This fierce attraction was nothing more than the product of their secret love affair. Anticipation of the moment they'd finally connect, laced with a hint of the forbidden. It had colored everything and she refused to fall prey to manufactured expectations about what was happening between them.

Get a grip. "Smells like ham and biscuits," she said brightly.

He handed her the bag. "I hope you like them. I had to drive two towns over to find them."

The first bite of biscuit hit her tongue and she moaned. "I would have paid three hundred euros for this."

He laughed. "On the house. You can pay next time."

"Oh?" She arched a brow, relieved they'd settled

back into the teasing, fun vibe she'd liked about them from the beginning. "Are you under some mistaken impression that I'm a liberated woman who insists on opening her own doors and paying her own way? 'Cause that is so not happening."

"My mistake," he allowed smoothly with a nod and munched on his own biscuit. "You want a manly bloke to treat you like a delicate hothouse flower. I get it. I'd be chuffed to climb all the ladders around here and wield the power tools in order to create a luxury hideaway, as ordered. You know what that means I get at the end of the day in return, right?"

"A full body massage," she guessed, already planning exactly how such a reward might play out. "And then some inventive foreplay afterward."

That was even more fun to imagine than the massage part of the evening's agenda.

"Oh, no, sweetheart." He leaned in and tipped her chin up to capture her gaze, and the wicked intent written all over his face made her shiver. "It means I get the loo first."

Eight

The farmhouse's great room looked brand-new and James couldn't take all of the credit. It was because the house had good bones and old-world charm—qualities he'd never appreciated in anything before.

Hell, maybe he'd never even *noticed* them before.

Bella finished polishing the last silver candlestick and stuck it back on the mantel of the humongous fireplace, humming a nameless tune that he'd grown a bit fond of over the past day as they'd worked side by side to get their lover's retreat set to rights.

"Did you hear that?" she asked with a cocked head.

"Uh, no." He'd been too busy soaking in the

sight of a beautiful woman against the backdrop of the deep maroon walls and dark furniture. "What was it?"

"The sound of success."

She smiled and that heavy feeling in his chest expanded a tad more, which had been happening with alarming frequency all day. Unfortunately, the coping mechanism he'd used last night—grabbing Bella and sinking into her as fast as possible so his mind went blessedly blank—wasn't available to him at this moment because a workman from the municipality was on his way to restore the water connection.

It was a minor miracle the workman had come out on short notice, given the typical local bureaucracy, but once James had mentioned that he was a representative for the Montoros, everything had fallen into place.

He'd have to make himself—and his distinctive green car—scarce. Just as he'd done this morning when the bloke from the electric company had come. But it was fine. The time away had given him an opportunity to talk through strategy with his sports agent, who mentioned a possible opportunity with Liverpool. No guarantees, but some shifting had occurred in the roster and the club needed a strong foot. Brilliant news at an even better time—the sooner James could escape Alma, the better.

"Yep," he said and cleared a catch from his throat. "Only twenty-seven rooms to go."

They'd started on the downstairs, focusing on the kitchen and great room, plus the servant's quarters past the kitchen, where they intended to sleep tonight if the bed they'd ordered arrived on time, as promised. A lot had been accomplished in one day but not nearly enough.

Once they got the master bedroom upstairs cleaned up, James planned a whole silk-sheets-and-rose-petals-type seduction scene. He owed it to Bella since she'd been such a good sport about sleeping in the room designated for the help.

One thing he immensely appreciated about Bella: she joked around a lot about being high maintenance but she was the furthest thing from it. And he knew a difficult, demanding woman when he saw one, like his last semipermanent girlfriend, Chelsea. She'd cured him of ever wanting to be around a female for more than a one-night stand, a rule which he'd stuck to for nearly two years.

Until Bella.

Since he couldn't lose his mind in her fragrant skin for…he glanced at his watch and groaned… hours, he settled for a way-too-short kiss.

She wiggled away and stuck her tongue out at him. "Yes, we have a lot of work left. But not as much as we would have if you hadn't made all those calls. You're the main reason we've gotten this far."

The hero-worship in her gaze still made him uncomfortable, so he shrugged and polished an already-sparkling crystal bowl with the hem of his shirt so he had an excuse not to look directly at her. "Yeah, that was a brilliant contribution. Hitting some numbers on my phone."

"Stop being such a goof." Hands on her hips, she stepped into his space, refusing to let his attention linger elsewhere. "You're a great person. I'm allowed to think so and don't you dare tell me I can't."

That pulled a smile from him. "Yes, Your Highness."

"Anyway," she drawled with an exaggerated American accent, which only widened his smile, as she'd probably intended. "When I was cleaning the fireplace, I realized I really need to call my father. We can't ignore the press release about my engagement to Will much longer."

Though she kept up her light tone, he could tell some stress had worked its way into her body. Her shoulders were stiff and a shadow clouded her normally clear eyes.

"Maybe we can wait," he suggested, and laced his fingers with hers to rub her knuckles. "Tomorrow's soon enough."

"I kind of want to get it over with." She bit her lip, clearly torn. "But I also really like the idea of procrastinating."

"Why?" he asked, surprising himself. He'd meant to say they should wait. Why do today what you can put off until tomorrow?

He, of all people, understood avoiding conflict, especially when it involved an overbearing father. But the distress evident in the foreign lines around her eyes had to go and he would do whatever it took to solve the problem.

Maybe it wasn't a good thing for him to encourage her to wait. Maybe she needed to get the confrontation over with. But how would he know if he didn't ask?

"My father really wants me to fall in line, like Gabriel did. When Rafe abdicated, it was kind of a big deal." She sighed. "I get that. I really don't want to cause problems because of my own self-ishness."

"But you're not," he countered. "How is it a problem that you want to choose the bloke you marry?"

"Because my father says it is." Her mouth flattened into a grim line. "That's why I want to put off dealing with all of this. I'm just not ready for all of the expectations that go along with restoring the monarchy. I mean, I always knew our family had come from a royal line, but that was so long ago. Why is it so important to my father all of a sudden?"

She seemed a little fragile in that moment so he pulled her into his arms, shushing her protests over the state of her cleanliness.

"I wish I could tell you why things are important to fathers," he murmured. "Mine has yet to explain why it's so horrifying to him that I don't want a job at Rowling Energy. Becoming a world-class football player might make some dads proud."

"Not yours?" she whispered, her head deep in his shoulder.

Her arms tightened around him, which was oddly comforting. What had started as an embrace he'd thought she needed swiftly became more precious to him than oxygen.

"Nah. Will's his golden boy."

"Why don't you want to work at Rowling?"

It was the first time anyone had ever asked him that.

Most people assumed he wanted to play football and there was little room for another career at his dad's company. But even now, when he had few choices in continuing his sports career, he'd never consider Rowling an alternative.

His father wasn't the listening type; he just bull-dozed through their conversations with the mindset that James would continue to defy him and never bothered to wonder why James showed no interest in the family business.

"It's because he built that company on my mother's grave," he said fiercely. "If she hadn't died, he wouldn't have moved to Alma and tapped in to the offshore drilling that was just starting up. I can't ever forget that."

"Is someone asking you to forget?" she probed quietly. "Maybe there's room to take a longer view of this. If your father hadn't moved to Alma, you wouldn't have discovered that you loved football, right?"

"That doesn't make it okay." The admission reverberated in the still house and she lifted her head to look at him, eyebrows raised in question. "I love football but only because it saved me. It got me out of Alma at an early age and gave me the opportunity to be oceans away. I can't be on the same small island as my father. Not for long."

When had this turned into confession time? He'd never said that out loud before. Bella had somehow pulled it out of him.

"I'm sorry," she said quietly and snuggled back into his arms, exactly where he wanted her.

"I'm sorry you've got the same issues with your father. But there's always gossip in a small town. We're going to be dealing with a scandal over the press release once someone catches on to us shacking up in this love nest. But I support whatever decision you make as far as the timing," he told her sincerely, though he'd be heavily in favor of waiting.

He wasn't royalty though. She had a slew of obligations he knew nothing about; he could hardly envision a worse life than one where you had to think about duty to crown and country.

"I think that's the most romantic thing you've ever said to me." Her voice cracked on the last word.

Puzzled, he tipped her chin up, and a tear tracked down her cheek. "Which part? When I called this jumble of a house a love nest or described our relationship as shacking up?"

She laughed through another couple of tears, thoroughly confounding him. Just when he thought he finally got her, she did something he couldn't fathom.

"Neither. The part where you said you support me, no matter what. It makes me warm, right here." She patted her stomach.

He almost rolled his eyes. That was laying it on a bit thick, wasn't it? "I do support you, but that's what peop—lovers…people in a rela—" God, he couldn't even get his tongue to find the right word to explain the status of what they were doing here.

Maybe because he didn't *know* what they were doing here.

"Yeah," she said happily, though what she was agreeing to, he had no idea. "That's what you do. I get that. You've always done exactly the right thing, from the very beginning. "

He scowled. "I don't do that."

He didn't. He was the guy who buckled when it mattered most. The guy whose team had been counting on him and he'd let them down. The guy who ran from conflict instead of dealing with it. Hadn't she been listening to anything he'd said about why he played football?

His character had been tarnished further with the hooker incident. James Rowling was the last person anyone should count on. Especially when it came to support. Or "being there" for someone emotionally.

"You do." Her clear blue eyes locked with his and she wouldn't let him look away. "You look in the mirror and see the mistakes your father has insisted you've made. I look at you and see an amazing man. You did hard physical labor all day in a house that means nothing to you. Because I asked you to. You're here. That means a lot to me. I need a rock in my life."

She had him all twisted up in her head as the hero of this story. She couldn't be more wrong— he was a rock, all right. A rolling stone headed for the horizon.

It suddenly sounded lonely and unappetizing. "I can't be anyone's rock. I don't know how."

That had come out wrong. He intended to be firm and resolute, but instead sounded far too harsh.

"Oh, sweetie. There's no instruction manual. You're already doing it." She shook her head and feathered a thumb over his jaw in a caress that felt more intimate than the sex they'd had last night. "You're letting someone else cloud your view of yourself. Don't let your father define who you are."

He started to protest and then her words really sank in. Had he subconsciously been doing that— letting his father have that much power over him?

Maybe he'd never realized it because he'd refused to admit the rift between him and his father might be partially his own fault. James had always been too busy running to pay attention. Even now, his thoughts were on Liverpool and the potential opportunity to play in the top league. But more importantly, Liverpool wasn't in Alma—where the woman who had him so wrongly cast in her head as the hero lived. He was thinking about leaving. Maybe he was already halfway out the door.

Which then begged the question—what if he buckled under pressure because he always took off when the going got tough?

The new bed was supremely superior to the floor. Bella and James christened it that night and slept entwined until morning. It was the best night of sleep she'd ever had in her life.

But dawn brought a dose of reality. She hadn't been back to the Playa del Onda house in almost forty-eight hours. The quick text message to Gabriel to explain her absence as a "getaway with a friend" hadn't stopped her father from calling four times and leaving four terse voice mail messages. She hadn't answered. On purpose.

With the addition of running water and electricity, the farmhouse took on a warmth she enjoyed. In fact, she'd rather stay here forever than go back to the beach house. But she had to deal with her father eventually. If this matter of the engagement announcement was simply a test of her father's resolve versus her own, she wouldn't care very much about the scandal of being with James.

But it wasn't just about two Montoros squaring off against each other. It was a matter of national alliances and a fledgling monarchy. She didn't have any intention of marrying Will, but until the Montoros issued a public retraction of the engagement story, the possibility of another scandal was very real. This one might be far worse for Gabriel on the heels of the one Rafe had caused. And hiding away with James hadn't changed that. She had to take care of it. Soon.

"Good morning," James murmured and reached out to stroke hair from her face as he lay facing her on the adjacent pillow. "This is my favorite look on you."

"Bedhead?" She smiled despite the somberness of her thoughts.

"Well loved." He grinned back. "I liked it yesterday morning, too."

Speaking of which… "How long do you think we can reasonably hole up here without someone snapping a picture of us together?"

He shrugged one shoulder. "Forever." When she arched a brow, he grinned. "I can fantasize about that, can't I? As long as I keep jetting off when people show up, what's the hurry?"

Her conscience pricked at her. James was leaving the timing of forcing the issue to her, but a scandal could be damaging to him as well. It was selfish enough to refuse to marry Will, but she wasn't really hurting him as long as they were up front about it. A scandal that broke before the retraction could very well hurt James and she couldn't stand that.

"I think I need to talk to my father today," she said firmly. "Or tomorrow at the very latest."

James deserved what he'd asked for—the right to take her out in public, to declare to the world that they'd started seeing each other. To take her to a hotel, or dinner or wherever he liked. It wasn't fair to force him to help her clean up this old farmhouse just so she could avoid a confrontation.

Except she wasn't only avoiding the confrontation. She was avoiding admitting to herself that her own desires had trumped her responsibilities. Hurricane Bella had followed her across the Atlantic after all.

"I'll drive you back to Playa Del Onda," he said immediately. "Whenever you're ready."

A different fear gripped her then. What if they got everything straightened out and she and James could be together with no fear of scandal—only for her to discover things between them were so amazing because of the extreme circumstances? The white-hot attraction between them might fizzle if their secret affair wasn't so secret any longer.

That was enough to change her mind.

"I'll probably never be ready. Let's shoot for tomorrow." That was too soon. The thought of losing her allure with James made her want to weep. "Let's get some more work on the house done today. It'll give me time to gear up. Is that okay? Do you have something else you need to be doing?"

"Nothing I would rather be doing, that's for sure. I'm completely open."

"Me, too."

And for some reason, that didn't sit well, as if she was some kind of Eurotrash princess who had nothing better to do than lie around all day getting it on with a hot athlete. That was like a tabloid story in and of itself.

The urn from the great room popped into her

head. Usefulness created worth and she wanted to feel that her life had worth.

"You know what I'd like to do?" she said impulsively. "Find out if there's a wildlife conservation organization in Alma."

James, to his credit, didn't register a lick of surprise. "I'll help you find one."

Of course he'd say that, without questioning why. His unwavering support was fast becoming a lifeline. "I was involved in one back in Miami. I like taking care of poor, defenseless creatures. Especially birds. We had wild macaws on the grounds at our house and I always felt like they were there as a sign. I miss them. I miss feeling like I'm doing something to give back, you know?"

"It's a good cause," he agreed. "There are some estuaries on the east side of the main island. Lots of migratory birds and fish live there. Surely there are some organizations devoted to their preservation. If not, you're in the perfect position to start one."

Her breath caught. At last, a use for the title of princess. If her brother was running the show, he could give her backing in parliament to get some state money set aside. Fund-raisers galore could come out of that. "Thanks. I love that idea."

"If we're going to Playa Del Onda tomorrow, you want to swing by the Playa branch of the Ministry of Agriculture and Environment and see if they have any information on wildlife conservation?"

"Definitely. And then I'd like to come back and put together a serious renovation plan for the house. But I'm not suggesting you have to help," she amended in a rush.

Good grief. Everything that came out of her mouth sounded as if she was ordering him around, expecting him to play chauffer and be a general Alma guide. He might have his own life to live. Or he might realize the thrill had worn off.

"I want to help," he insisted. "My assumption is that we're still planning to lie low, even after you clear things up with your father. So that means we need a place to go. I like it here."

She let out the breath caught in her lungs. She shouldn't read into his response. But for some reason, it made her feel a little better that he wasn't already planning to ditch their relationship once it wasn't secret any longer. "I do, too."

She'd started thinking she might like to live in

the farmhouse permanently. It wasn't too far from Del Sol, so she could visit Tía Isabella occasionally. If she planned to stay in Alma, she had to live *somewhere*. Why not here? No one else cared about it.

As she lay in the bed James had ordered and smiled at him in the early morning light, it occurred to her that *he* was the only reason she'd even thought about a permanent place to live. As if James and forever were intertwined.

That was enough to propel her from the bed with a quickly tossed-off excuse about taking a shower now that she could.

As the water heated up, she berated herself for dreaming about life beyond the next few days. It was one thing to question whether James would lose interest once they could go public with their affair, but it was another entirely to assign him a permanent place in her life without even consulting him.

What would his place be? Boyfriend? Official lover? She'd be living in the public eye far more in Alma than in Miami. What if James didn't want that kind of scrutiny? She wouldn't blame him, especially given the past scandals that dogged his steps.

Of course, she didn't know his thoughts one way or another. Maybe he'd be done with their affair in a few days, regardless of the status of their relationship. Maybe the whole concept of being her long-term lover had little appeal.

What was she *thinking*?

What had happened to the girl who used to flit from one guy to the next with ease? Or for that matter, the girl who flitted from party to party? Living out here in the country would make it really difficult to stay in the scene. No jetting off to Monte Carlo or Barcelona for some fun on the Mediterranean when Alma grew too dull. But when she exited the bathroom and saw the beautiful, surprisingly romantic man still in the bed they'd shared last night, sprawled out under the covers like a wicked fantasy, all of that drained from her mind. What party—what other man, for that matter—could compare to *that*?

"Give me a few minutes and we'll get started," he promised. "Let's check out the upstairs today."

God, she was in a lot of trouble. *She* should be

the one thinking about cooling things off, not wor-rying about whether James planned to.

But the thought of ending things with James made her nauseous.

What was she going to do?

Nine

The upstairs master suite had the most amazing four-poster bed Bella had ever seen. When she drew off the drop cloths covering it, she almost gasped at the intricate carvings in the wood. Delicate flowers in full bloom twined up the posts and exploded into bunches at the top corners.

Once she polished the wood to gleaming and whacked the dust from the counterpane and pillows, the bed took on an almost magical quality, as if it had been a gift from the fairy realm to this one.

The rest of the room was a wreck. Mice had gotten into the cushions of the chairs by the huge bay window and Bella could tell by the discoloration of the walls that some type of artwork had originally hung there, but had disappeared at some point over the years.

The floor groaned behind her and she turned to see James bouncing lightly on a spot near the bed. The planks bowed under his weight and then with a *snap*, one cracked in two. Both pieces fell into the newly created hole. It was a testament to James's superior balance and athletic reflexes that the broken plank hadn't thrown him to the floor.

"Oops," he said sheepishly as he leaped clear. "I was not expecting that to happen. Sorry."

She waved it off. "If that's the worst damage we do today, I'll consider that a plus. Why, exactly, were you jumping up and down on it in the first place?"

"When I walked over it, this section felt different, like it wasn't solid underneath. It turns out it wasn't."

Grinning at his perplexed expression, she joined him to peer into the hole. It was a shallow compartment, deliberately built into the floor. "Looks like you found the royal hiding place. Oooh, maybe there are still some priceless jewels in there."

Eagerly, she knelt and pulled the broken board from the hole. "Hand me your phone."

James placed it in her outstretched hand and when she aimed it into the gap, the lighted screen revealed a small box. Leaning forward slightly on her knees, she stuck her hand down into the space and only as her fingers closed over the box did she think about the possibility of spiders. Ick. Since it was too late, she yanked the box out and set it on the floor next to James.

"Anything else?" he asked, his body hot against her back as he peered over her shoulder, lips grazing her ear.

It shouldn't have been such a turn-on, but then, there was nothing about James that *didn't* turn her on. Warmth bloomed in her midsection and as she arched her back to increase the contact with his torso, the feel of him hummed through her.

"Maybe," she murmured. "Why don't you reach around here and see for yourself."

He must have picked up on her meaning. His arms embraced her from behind, drawing her backward into his body, and his fingers fumbled around the edge of the hole without delving more than half an inch into it.

"Nope. Nothing in there." His lips nuzzled her neck as he spoke and she could tell his attention was firmly on her. The hard length grinding into her rear said he'd lost interest in whatever else might be in the decades-old hiding place as well. "But what have we here?"

"I think you better investigate," she said, and guided his hands under her shirt, gasping as his questing fingertips ran over her sensitive breasts.

"You're not fully dressed," he accused her with a naughty laugh. "Ms. Montoro, I am shocked at your lack of undergarments. It's almost as if you expected a bloke's hands to be under your shirt."

"You say that like it's a bad thing." Her core heated as he caressed her, nudging her rear with his hard erection. "And as you're the only man around, you're welcome."

His laugh vibrated along her spine, warming her further. She loved it when he laughed, loved being the reason he was amused. Loved it when he touched her as if he'd discovered something rare and precious and he planned to become intimately familiar with every nook and cranny.

Then he got serious, palming her aching nipples, massaging and working her flesh until she could hardly breathe from wanting him. Would she *ever* get tired of that, of the gasping need and clawing desire? She hoped not.

She whipped off her shirt and tossed it on the bed, granting him full access. Arching against him, she pushed her breasts into his hands and flung her head back against his shoulder. As if reading her mind, he fastened his lips to her earlobe, sucking on it gently as one hand wandered south in a lazy pattern, pouring more fire on top of the flames he'd already ignited as her flesh heated under his fingertips.

Finally, his fingers slid into her shorts and toyed for an eternity with her panties, stroking her through the fabric, teasing her as he kissed her throat. So hot and ready, she could hardly stand waiting until he'd had his fill of exploring.

When she moaned in protest at the delay, he eased her back against his thighs and slipped off the rest of her clothing. Without a word, he picked her up and spun her around, placing her gently on the bed, his dark gaze worshipping her body.

Even that heaped more coals on the fire and she shuddered.

Through hazy vision, she watched as he knelt between her thighs and kissed each one. His tongue traced a straight line across her flesh and then he glanced up at her under his lashes as he licked her core. His tongue was hard and blistering hot and wet.

The flare of white-hot pleasure made her cry out. He dove in, tasting her in a sensuous perusal that drained her mind. *Yes*, she screamed. Or maybe that had only been in her head. Her body thrashed involuntarily as he pleasured her with his mouth, slight five o'clock shadow abrading her thighs as he moved.

Higher and higher she spun, hips bucking closer to the source of this amazing pleasure with each thrust of his tongue. The light scape of his teeth against her sensitive bud set off a rolling, thick orgasm that blasted her apart faster and harder than anything she'd ever felt before.

"Now," she murmured huskily and lay back on the counterpane in invitation. "I want your very fine body on mine."

He complied, clothes hitting the floor in a moment. He stretched out over her, his lean torso brushing her breasts deliciously. She wiggled until they were aligned the way she wanted, reveling in the dark sensation of this man covering her.

Savoring the anticipation, she touched him, letting her hands roam where they pleased. Fingertips gliding over his muscled back—gorgeously bunching as he held himself erect so he wouldn't crush her—she hummed her appreciation and nipped at his lips until he took her mouth in a scorching kiss reminiscent of the one he'd given her at her core, tongue deep inside her.

Wordlessly, she urged him on by rolling her hips, silently begging him to complete her as only he could. A brief pause as he got the condom on and then he slid into her, filling her body as gloriously as he filled her soul.

She gasped and clung with all her muscles.

James.

Absolutely the best thing that had ever happened to her. The sexiest man she'd ever been with, for sure, but also the only one who *saw* her. No pretense. No games. She couldn't tear her gaze from his face and something shifted inside, opening the floodgates of a huge and wonderful and irrevocable surge of emotion.

She let herself feel, let everything flow as he

loved her. She couldn't even find the capacity to be shocked. It was dangerous—she knew that—but couldn't help it. Murmuring encouragement, his name, who knew what else, she rode out another climax made all the more intense by the tenderness blooming in her heart for the man who'd changed everything. But the wonderful moment soured as soon as her breathing slowed and the hazy glow wore off. She couldn't tell him she'd discovered all these things inside that had his name written all over them. Could she?

No. Fear over his reaction gripped her and in the end, she kept her big mouth shut. After their affair became public, maybe she could admit he'd done something irrevocable to her. But now, reeling it all back, she lay in his arms, letting him hold her tight as if he never meant to let go.

Later, when they'd finally gained the strength to dress, she noticed the box still on the floor near the broken boards. "We should open that."

She pushed at it with her bare foot and it tumbled over, lid flying open and spilling its contents all over the hardwood planks. Letters. Ten or twenty of them, old and fragile, with spidery pale blue handwriting looping across the yellowed pages.

Picking one up, she squinted at it but in the low light of the still musty bedroom, it was too hard to read. She flipped it over to see more of the same faded writing.

"What are they?" James peered over her shoulder, breath warm and inviting across her neck. "Front *and* back. Looks like someone had a lot to say."

"Oh, no." She shook her head and moved out of his reach with a laugh that came out a lot less amused than she'd intended. "You are banned from coming up behind me from now on."

She was far too raw inside to let him open her up again. Not so soon.

"What?" His wicked grin belied the innocent spread of his hands. "I was curious. I can't help it if breathing the same air as me gets you all hot and bothered."

It was a perfectly legitimate thing to say. They flirted and teased each other all the time. *All* the time, and she normally loved it.

He was just so beautiful standing there against the backdrop of the bed where he'd made her feel amazing and whole, made her feel as if she could do anything as long as he was by her side, holding her hand.

Suddenly, her throat closed and she barely caught a sob that welled up from nowhere. This was supposed to be a fun-filled, magnificently hot getaway from the world. When had everything gotten so complicated?

"I, um… Tía Isabella will want these." Bella held up the letters in one hand with false cheer. "I'm just going to go put them in my bag so I don't forget them."

She turned away from James and left the room as quickly as she could without alerting him to her distress. Apparently she'd succeeded.

And now she was completely messed up because she'd hoped he would follow her and demand to know why she was crying.

They slept in the servant's quarters again because they hadn't gotten nearly enough accomplished upstairs due to the detour Bella had sprung on James.

Not that he minded. She could detour like that all day long.

When he awoke, he missed Bella's warmth instantly. She wasn't in the bed. Sitting up, he sought a glimpse of her through the open bathroom door, but nada.

Shame. He liked waking up with her hair across his chest and her legs tangled with his. Surprisingly. This was officially the longest stretch he'd spent with a woman in…ages. Not since Chelsea. And even then, he hadn't been happy in their relationship, not for a long time. When she'd broken up with him because she'd met someone else, he'd been relieved.

Wondering where Bella had taken off to, James vaulted from the bed and dressed, whistling aimlessly as he stuck his shirt over his head. He felt a twinge in his back at the site of an old football injury. Probably because he'd spent the past few days using a different muscle group than the ones he normally engaged while strength training and keeping his footwork honed. Cleaning decades of grime from a place was hard work. But he liked the result—both in the appearance of the house and the gratitude Bella expressed.

Strolling out into the newly-scrubbed kitchen, he reached for the teapot he'd purchased, along with a slew of other absolute necessities, and saw Bella in his peripheral vision sitting outside on the back stoop. She was staring off into the distance as if something was troubling her.

He had a suspicion he knew what it was. Today they were supposed to drive into Playa Del Onda. Should he pretend he'd forgotten and not bring it up so they didn't have to go? He hated that she'd worked the whole confrontation over the engagement announcement up in her mind into something unpleasant. It really shouldn't be so complicated.

Demand a retraction. Done. Of course, getting her father to agree wouldn't necessarily be easy, but it certainly wouldn't be complicated.

In the end, he opted to join her on the stoop without comment, drawing her into his arms to watch the sun burst from behind the clouds to light up the back acreage. She snuggled into his torso and they sat companionably, soaking up the natural beauty of the wild overgrowth.

A horn blasted from the front of the house, startling them both. "Expecting someone?" he asked and she shook her head. "Stay here. I'll see what it is."

"You can't." Her mouth turned down. "I have to be the one. It's Montoro property."

Enough of this hiding and watching their step and having to do things separately so no one could take a picture of them together. They were catering to the whims of their fathers, whether she realized it or not.

"We'll go together." He rose and held out his hand.

She hesitated for so long, an uneasy prickle skittered across the back of his neck. It was way past time to dispense with all this secrecy nonsense. He wanted to do what he pleased and go wherever he wished without fear of someone creating a scandal. Today was a perfect day to stop the madness, since they already planned to confront her father.

Firmly, he took her hand and pulled her to her feet. "Yes. Together. If someone takes a picture, so be it. We're talking to your father today, so there's no reason to keep up this game of hide and seek. Not any longer."

Heaving a huge breath, she nodded. "Okay."

Together, they walked to the front, where a delivery driver stood on the front drive, waving.

"Tengo un paquete," he said, and touched his cap.

Smashing. One-day delivery, as advertised.

James had been worried the gift he'd ordered for Bella wouldn't arrive in time, but obviously the exorbitant rush charge had been worth it.

"*Gracias*," James responded immediately. *"¿Dónde firmo?"*

Bella's eyebrows quirked. "When did you learn Spanish?"

"In like grade four," he retorted with a laugh. "I grew up in a Spanish-speaking country, remember?"

The driver held out his clipboard and once James signed, the deliveryman went to the back of the truck and pulled free a large parcel. Handing it over, the driver nodded once and climbed back into his truck, starting it up with a roar.

The package squawked over the engine sound.

"What in the world is in there?" Bella asked, clearly intrigued as James carried the box into the house through the front door, careful not to cover the air holes with his arms.

"It's a gift. For you." James pulled the tab to open the top of the box, as the Spanish instructions indicated. The box side fell open to reveal the large metal birdcage holding two green macaws. They squawked in tandem.

Bella gasped. "James! What is this?"

"Well, I must have gotten the wrong birds if it's not abundantly clear," he said wryly. "You said you missed your macaws so I brought some to you. Are they okay?"

He'd paid an additional flat fee to guarantee the birds would arrive alive. They looked pretty chipper for having been shipped from the mainland overnight.

With a loud sniff and a strange, strangled mumble, Bella whirled and fled the room, leaving James with two loud birds and a host of confusing, unanswered questions.

"I guess I muddled things up," he told the birds.

He put the cage on the coffee table and gave them some water as he'd been instructed when he ordered the birds, but his irritation rose as he poured. More water ended up on the floor than in the container.

If he could just punch something, his mood would even out. Probably.

Was he supposed to chase Bella down and apologize for spending money on her? Demand an explanation for why she'd hated the gift so much, a simple thank you was beyond her?

By the time he'd ripped open the package of bird food and poured some in the dish, she hadn't returned and his temper had spiked past the point of reasonableness. So he went in search of her and found her upstairs lying in a tight ball on the bed in the master suite. Sobbing.

Instantly, his ire drained and he crawled into the bed to cuddle her, stroking her hair until she quieted enough to allow his windpipe to unclench. "What's wrong, sweetheart?"

She didn't answer and his gut twisted.

Maybe she'd been looking for the exit and his gift had upset her. Women were funny about expensive presents, thinking a bloke had all kinds of expectations in mind if they accepted the gift.

"There aren't any strings attached to the birds, Bella. If you like them, keep them. If you don't, I'll…" *No returns*, the place had said. "…sort it."

His throat went tight again. If she was done here, the birds were the least of his problems. He wasn't ready to end things, not yet. Eventually, sure. His agent had a phone call scheduled with Liverpool today, but that was only the beginning of a long process that might not net him anything other than dashed hopes.

Had he inadvertently speeded up the timeline of their parting with his gesture?

"I like them," she whispered, her mouth buried in the bedspread.

His heart unstuck from his rib cage and began to beat again. "Then talk to me, hon. I'll uncomplicate it, whatever it is."

Without warning, she flipped to face him and the ravaged look on her face sank hooks into his stomach, yanking it toward his knees.

"Not this. You can't uncomplicate it because *you're* the complication, James."

Circles again, and they didn't do circles. Not normally. She shot straight—or at least she had thus far. Had things changed so much so quickly?

"What did I do that's so horrible?" he demanded.

The little noise of disgust she made deep in her throat dredged up some of his earlier temper, but he bit it back to give her the floor.

"You came in here," she raged, "and tore down all my ideas about how this thing between us was going to go. You understand me, pay attention to me. And worse than all of that, you made me fall for you!"

The starkness in her expression sealed his mouth

shut once and for all, and he couldn't have spoken for a million euros.

"And I'm scared!" she continued. "I've never been in love. What am I supposed to do? Feel? I'm running blindfolded through the dark."

Too much. Too fast. Too...everything. He blinked rapidly but it didn't do anything to ease the burning in his eyes. He couldn't...she wasn't... *Deep breath. Hold it together.*

She was afraid. Of *him* and what was happening inside her. That was the most important thing to address first. Cautiously, he reached out and took her hand. He was so completely out of his depth, it was a wonder his brain hadn't shut down.

This was a challenge. Maybe the most important one of his life, and after all his claims of being able to uncomplicate anything, now was a good time to start. No buckling under the pressure allowed. Bella needed to feel as if she could trust him and obviously she didn't.

Heart pounding—because honestly, the freaking out wasn't just on her side—he cleared his throat. "Look me in the eye and tell me that again. But without all the extra stuff."

"Which part?" she whispered, searching his gaze, her eyes huge, their expression uneasy.

"The thing about falling for me." Her nails cut into his hand as they both tightened their grip simultaneously. This was a tipping point, and the next few minutes would decide which way it tipped. "I want to hear it straight from your heart."

His lungs seized and he honestly couldn't have said which way he wanted it to tip. What did he hope to accomplish by making this request of her? But he'd spoken the honest truth—regardless of everything, he wanted to hear it again.

"I'm falling for you," she said simply in the husky voice that automatically came out when she was deeply affected.

Something broke open inside him, washing him with warmth, huge and wonderful and irreversible. And suddenly, it wasn't very complicated at all. "Yeah. I've got something along those lines going on over here as well."

That something had been going on for a while. And he was quite disturbed that Will had realized it first. Bella was special and admitting it wasn't the big deal he'd made it out to be. Because the specialness had always been true, from the first moment her body aligned with his on the beach. It was as if he'd been waiting for that moment his whole life and when it happened, his world clicked into place.

"Really?" Hope sprang into her eyes, deepening the blue. "Like a little bit or a whole lot?"

"With no basis for comparison, I'd say it's something like being flung off a cliff and finding out exactly what maximum velocity is," he said wryly. "And it's about as scary as cliff diving with no parachute, since we're on the subject."

The smile blooming on her face reminded him of the sunrise they'd just watched together outside, before the birds had prompted this second round of confessions.

"Isn't it against the guy code to tell a woman she scares you?" She inched toward him and smoothed a hand over his upper arm, almost as if she was comforting him—which was supposed to be his role in this scenario.

"All of this is against the guy code." He rolled his eyes and she laughed, as he'd intended. The harmonious fullness in his chest that magically appeared at the sound was an unexpected bonus.

"Can you at least fill me in on why I had to pry all of this out of you with a crowbar?"

She scrubbed at her face, peering at him through her fingers. "This is not how it was supposed to go. We were going to have a couple of hot dates and maybe I would end up going back to Miami. Maybe you'd jet off to another country like you always do. No one said anything about losing my heart along the way."

A little awed at the thought of Bella's heart belonging to him, he reached out and flattened his palm against her chest, reveling in the feel of it beating against his hand. "I'll take good care of it."

He realized instantly that it was the wrong thing to say.

"For how long?" She sat up and his hand fell away. He missed the warmth immediately, "Until you get a new football contract and take off? You don't do relationships. *I* don't do relationships. Are you prepared to figure out why the hard way— with each other?"

"Yes," he said instantly. "Stop making this so difficult. *If* I get a contract, you come with me. Simple."

The alternative was unthinkable. Actually, he'd

never thought about these kinds of things. Never had a reason to. Women came, women left. But this one—he had an opportunity here to grab on to her tight with both hands and no matter how much it scared him, he wasn't letting go.

Catching her lip between her teeth, she worried it almost raw. "What if we get my father to retract the engagement announcement and everything is wonderful. We can date in the open. And then we find out the only thing we had going for us was the secrecy?"

"What, you're afraid I won't be keen on all of this if we don't have to sneak around?" A laugh slipped from his mouth before he fully registered the serious set of her jaw. It finally dawned on him. "That's what you're afraid of."

She shifted uncomfortably. "It's a real possibility."

"It's a real possibility that you'll figure out the same thing," he shot back and the wracked expression on her face floored him. "You already thought of that."

Ice formed instantly in his stomach. It had never occurred to him while they were confessing unexpected feelings that he hadn't actually removed the complications. The *real* complications might only be beginning. Falling for each other didn't magically make either of them relationship material and the potential to hurt each other was that much greater as a result.

Sometimes, no matter how much you practiced, you still missed the goal. And neither of them actually had much practice. What were the odds of success?

"Why do you think I got so upset?" she countered. "You're giving me everything I've ever wanted, and then you give me things I had no idea I wanted, and my heart does all this crazy stuff when you look at me, and when you kiss me it's like my life finally makes sense, and what if I'm the one who's building up this relationship into something mythical because I really like my men with a side of forbidden?"

"Okay, breathe."

He half laughed and ran a hand through his hair. This rated as the most honest conversation he'd ever had with a woman. And that made it all the more fascinating that he was still here, determined not to buckle. Bella was worth it.

She breathed. And then dropped the second bomb. "What if I want to get married someday? Is that potentially in the cards?"

He let the idea rattle around inside for a long moment, but it didn't completely unnerve him to consider it. He wasn't saying yes, but wasn't saying no.

"What if it is?" He captured her gaze and held it, refusing to let her look away, where she might miss the sincerity of what he was telling her. "Will that scare you as well?"

His brother had predicted that, too. Silently, he cursed himself and then his omniscient twin. Well, he hadn't proposed yet and no one was saying he would. Grandfather's watch still belonged to James. For now.

"More than I could possibly tell you," she admitted.

But she didn't have to tell him because he had a pretty good idea that the adrenaline racing around in his body closely matched what was going on with her.

"And," she continued swiftly, "I'm not saying that I will want to get married. To you or anyone. But what if I do?"

"You know what?" He tipped her chin up. "I think it's a safe bet that we have more going on here than a forbidden love angle. And I also think that no matter what, we can be honest with each other about what's going on, whether it's marriage or something else. I might be wrong, but I'm willing to take that risk. Are you?"

"Will you hold my hand?" she asked in a small voice. "When you're holding my hand, I feel like the world is a different place, like nothing bad could ever happen."

Yeah, he got that. If they could do this together, it might actually work.

Tenderly, he laced his fingers with hers and held on. "I'll never let go, not even when we hit the water. Jump with me, Bella."

Her smile pierced his heart and he started to believe they might figure this out after all. There were a lot of unknowns, sure, and they still had to sort their families—which wouldn't be as easy as he might be pretending. But it felt as if they were at the beginning of something wonderful.

It wasn't until they'd climbed into the Lamborghini an hour later that he glanced at his phone and noted two missed calls, followed by a text message…and had the strangest sense of foreboding, as if he'd vastly underestimated the level and complexity of the complications to come.

Ten

James was quiet during the drive back to Playa Del Onda and Bella left him alone with his thoughts.

After all, she'd been the one to change the game, and while he'd admitted his feelings had grown stronger than he'd expected as well, he hadn't argued when the subject of *what ifs* came up. It was a lot to take in. A lot to reconcile.

She still didn't know how she felt about all of this either. She certainly hadn't intended to blurt out something so difficult to take back as "I'm falling for you," but he'd been so sweet, first with the birds and then the way he handled her half-coherent stream of babbling about her fears. If any man was a keeper, it was James Rowling.

So the question was, how hard was it going to be to keep him? Her father was going to freak and there was no getting around the fact that James was still the wrong brother.

No matter. She wasn't ready to let James go, not yet. Whatever happened between her and James, they had a right to pursue it. And she wasn't leaving here without her father's promise to stop interfering.

When they walked into the house—together— Gabriel and her father were waiting for her in the foyer, thanks to a text message she'd sent on the way imploring her brother to play diplomat if the situation called for it.

Judging by the frown on Rafael's face, she'd made a good call.

"What is *he* doing here?" her father demanded, making it perfectly clear that he knew Bella hadn't brought home the correct Rowling despite their similar appearances—and that Rafael's feelings on the matter hadn't changed.

Bella halted but didn't drop James's hand. He squeezed hers tight in a show of solidarity but remained silent, earning a huge number of points. "James is here because I invited him. You've caused us both problems by announcing my engagement to Will Rowling and therefore, we both have a vested interest in resolving the situation."

"The problems caused by the engagement announcement are one hundred percent at your feet, Isabella." Her father crossed his arms over his expensive suit, presumably to ensure he appeared intimidating, but he'd lost any edge he might have had by using that tone of voice with her—and the man she was pretty sure she was in love with.

"Let's not sling accusations," Gabriel interjected and she smiled at him gratefully. "Listen to Bella, Dad. She's a grown woman and this is a friendly conversation between adults."

Rafael deflated. A bit.

Gabriel's "king" lessons had paid off, in Bella's humble opinion. He'd grown a lot in the past few weeks and no one was confused about Serafia's role in that. Her future sister-in-law—also the future queen—was an inspiration and Bella was happy to call Serafia family.

"You have the floor, Isabella." Her father glowered at James but didn't speak to him again, which was fine by her. For now.

"I don't want to marry Will. I told you this already. Why in the world would you go ahead and issue a press release saying we were engaged? Do you hate the idea of my happiness so much?" Her voice broke against her will.

Why did she still care so much that her father didn't seem to see her as anything other than a bargaining chip?

James stepped forward and addressed Rafael directly. "Sir, you don't know me and I realize I'm not your first choice for your daughter, but please understand that she makes me happy. I want nothing more than to do the same for her. I hope you can respect that."

Well, if there was any question about whether she was in love with him, that speech pretty much shot all doubt to hell. There might even be swooning in her future. She grinned at him, not even caring that she probably looked like a besotted fool.

Her father sighed and rubbed his head but before he could speak, Gabriel held out his hand to James, shaking it vigorously.

"I can respect that." Her brother nodded once at James. "I didn't get a chance to mention it when we first met, but I occasionally watched you play for Real Madrid. Bum deal that they released you. Big mistake on their part, in my opinion."

"Thanks." James smiled and bowed slightly to Gabriel, despite being told the prince didn't like formality. "And good luck to you. Alma is in brilliant hands with you at the helm."

Now that all the small talk was out of the way… "Dad, James and I are going to be a couple. You have to retract the engagement story or we're going to have a scandal on our hands. I don't want that for Gabriel or the Montoro family as a whole."

"All of which would have been avoided if you'd simply gotten with the program," Rafael insisted. "We're all making sacrifices for Gabriel—"

"Hold on a minute." The future king threw up his hands with a frown. "Don't drag me into this. I never asked Bella to marry Will Rowling and frankly, an arranged marriage is ridiculous in this day and age. I've never understood the reasoning."

"You need the alignment with Rowling Energy," her father sputtered and might have gone on if Gabriel hadn't interrupted again.

"Yes. I do. But Bella is asking us to find another way. What kind of king would I be if I didn't at least try to take her wishes into account?" Gabriel asked rhetorically, his regal voice echoing with sincerity in the grand foyer. "Dad, I think you should consider the retraction, especially if Bella and James's relationship is what they say it is."

Gabriel shot Bella a look that said he'd taken one look at her dopey face and made all kinds of assumptions about the nature of her relationship with James. But then, bringing James with her to the showdown had probably tipped her brother off to that the moment they'd crossed the threshold. "I don't kiss and tell, so you can forget any juicy details, if that's what you're after."

Gabriel mimed putting his fingers in his ears and shook his head with a shudder.

Clearing his throat in his no-nonsense way, Rafael put on his best disappointed-father face. "It's not just the alignment with Rowling Energy that's at stake here, Isabella. You have a tendency to be flighty. Irresponsible. Marriage will be good for you, if you choose someone who settles you. Will is as steady as they come."

The unvoiced and pointed barb directed at James was: *and the man you waltzed in here with is the opposite of steady.* The sting of hearing her father's unvarnished opinion of *her* was totally eclipsed by the negativity directed toward James, who was nothing like what her father assumed.

"That's where you're wrong, Dad. Will might be good at holding a company together, but James is good at holding *me* together. He settles me in a way I've never felt before. I'd rather spend an evening with him washing windows than at a party."

The words were out of her mouth before she consciously planned to say them, but once they took root in her heart, she recognized the truth. She didn't have any desire to be the party girl she'd been in Miami. Her boredom at Will Rowling's party hadn't had anything to do with the difference in party styles across the ocean, but in the subtle changes already happening inside *her*.

"By the way," she threw in. "You haven't asked, but in case you're wondering, your irresponsible daughter has spent the past few days restoring the old farmhouse near Aldeia Dormer that's part of the Montoro holdings. It looks really amazing so far and I couldn't have done it without James's help. I've also spent almost one hundred percent of that time with him, yet I dare you to find one illicit photograph of the two of us."

"What's this about a farmhouse?" Gabriel's eyebrows drew together as he homed in on her.

"I'll fill you in later," she promised. "Can you try to be happy for me, Dad? If you can't do that, I'll settle for that retraction. I do have a strong sense of my royal obligations. I'd just like you to respect the fact that I feel differently about what they are than you do."

"I'll issue the retraction but only to avoid the potential scandal. I cannot condone this relationship. I would prefer that you do not continue seeing him." Her father's sidelong glance at James spoke volumes. There was no doubt he still considered the wrong Rowling a terrible influence.

"I can't do that, Dad. And I'm disappointed that you still can't see the value James brings to my life." Her voice cracked and she cursed herself once again for caring. Regardless, she was getting the retraction she asked for, and she'd take it.

"You're right, I can't. I fully expect that once the thrill wears off, you'll be back to your former ways, Isabella." With that vote of no confidence ringing in her ears, her father motioned to James. "And if you're not, *he* will be. This is a disaster in the making. Will it do any good for me to warn you to keep your brother's reign at the forefront of your thoughts?"

"I always keep Gabriel in mind," she countered.

"Good, then the three of you can deal with Patrick Rowling." Her father wheeled on Gabriel with a scowl. "Since you're taking Bella's side in this, I'll let you handle the delicate matter of ensuring the alliance I painstakingly put into place won't suffer."

Her father stalked off to go terrorize the staff or something.

"Sorry," Bella said to her brother with a scowl. "I didn't mean for you to get in the middle of this. At least not that way. Are you okay with talking to Mr. Rowling?"

Unfortunately, thanks to the hours upon hours of conversation with James at the farmhouse, Bella knew exactly why Patrick wasn't going to be pleased with the developments.

"I'll talk to him," James volunteered, and Bella shot him a small smile.

"That's a good idea." Gabriel's expression reflected the gravity of the situation. "I'll speak with him as well. But it's sticky. We have business agreements in place that could be in jeopardy.

You should lie low for a while longer until matters are a bit more settled."

Great, more hiding. Why was it such a problem that two people wanted to spend time together? But the mention of things like business agreements clued her in that there was more at stake than she might have supposed.

At least her father hadn't forbidden her to see James. He just said he didn't want her to and made his disappointment in her clear. Fortunately, she had a lot of practice at living with her father's disappointment. If Gabriel worked things out with Mr. Rowling, maybe her father would come around. It could happen.

Gabriel and James talked a bit more about the logistics of their impending conversations with Patrick Rowling until James's cell phone rang.

He glanced at it and excused himself to take the call. Based on his expression, it must be shocking news indeed. Gabriel went off to do king stuff as James ended the call.

"What is it?" she whispered, almost afraid to ask. They'd barely confessed their fledgling feelings to each other, their fathers were still potential stumbling blocks in their relationship and she didn't know how many more hits they should be expected to take.

"Liverpool." His tone couldn't have been more stunned. "Management wants to meet with me. Tomorrow."

"Liverpool? Isn't that a city in England?" Then it dawned on her that he meant the football team. "They want to talk to you about a contract? That's great!"

"I have to fly to London." His enthusiasm shone from his face. Then he grew serious. "I don't know what they're going to say. But if it's an offer, it would be hard for me to turn down."

"Why would you turn it down? You can't."

"I would have to live in England for most of the year." His gorgeous eyes sought and held hers as the implications weighed down her shoulders.

This was serious, life-altering stuff, the kind of thing couples with a future considered. While she thought that was where they were headed—thought that was where she *wanted* them to go—it was another matter entirely to have Big Decisions dropped in your lap before you were ready. It was far scarier than accidentally revealing your feelings.

"We'll figure it out," she murmured, as though

she knew what she was talking about. "We're jumping together. Just don't let go of my hand, remember?"

Instead of agreeing, or grabbing her hand and shooting her a tender smile, he scrubbed at his eyes with stiff fingers. "Everything is moving too fast."

Her heart froze.

Everything? As in their relationship, too? He'd volunteered to come with her, to talk to his father and work out the issues between the Montoro family and Rowling Energy—was he having second thoughts now? "One step at a time, James. Go to England and see what they say. Then we can talk."

He nodded and swept her up in a fierce hug. She inhaled his familiar scent, soaked in his essence. That at least felt somewhat normal and it calmed her a bit.

"I'll call you the moment I know something. Guess I'll be gone a couple of days."

Watching him drive away wrenched something loose inside her and the place ached where it used to be attached. She rubbed at her chest and perversely wondered if it would get better or worse if he called with the news that Liverpool wanted to sign him. Because that's when she'd find out once and for all whether removing the temptation of the forbidden caused him to completely lose interest.

James resisted pulling at his starched collar. Barely. If he'd had more notice that Liverpool wanted a meeting, he might have scared up a more comfortable suit. Contract negotiations rarely included the player and the fact that Liverpool specifically asked for James to attend meant...what? He didn't know and it was weighing on him.

The small room got smaller the longer Liverpool's management murmured behind their cupped hands. James could tell from their less-than-impressed faces that his agent's opening pitch hadn't won anyone over.

So maybe the comfort of the suit didn't matter when your entire future was on the line.

Liverpool had expressed definite interest in picking up James if the price was right, according to his agent, but they wanted to move fast on making a decision.

James was not leaving here without that contract. It wasn't about the money. It was about putting his mistakes behind him and gaining the opportunity to prove his loyalty to a club. He had to. To show

Bella he was really the hero material she saw him as. To prove that he was worth all the trouble they'd gone through to be together.

James cleared his throat. "It's obvious you have reservations about me. What are your concerns?"

The three suits on the other side of the table all stared at him with varying degrees of surprise. Why, because he didn't subscribe to the British philosophy of keeping a stiff upper lip?

His sports agent, Spencer Stewart, shot him an annoyed glance and waved off James. "No one has reservations. We're all professionals here. So, give us your best offer and we'll consider it."

"Yes, we're all professionals," James agreed. "But these gentlemen have every right to question my capacity to act professionally. Let's call a spade a spade. I made mistakes. But I'm ready to be serious about my career and I want to play my heart out for a team willing to give me that chance."

All at once, it occurred to him that Alma's reserve team had already offered him that chance. And he'd turned his nose up at it. As if he was too good for what he considered the small time.

That didn't sit well. No club *owed* him a spot on the roster.

Liverpool's manager nodded slowly. "That's fair. As is our original salary offer. The cap is a concern, after all."

James kept his face straight, wishing he could argue. The cap was only a concern for a risky acquisition. They'd gladly pay the fines for going over the cap to gain a player with a less scandalous past. He'd have to take a pay cut if he wanted to play for Liverpool—and work twice as hard to earn it. Simple as that.

And he'd have to move to England.

A few days ago, he would have already been packed in anticipation of relocating as fast as possible. He could avoid his father for good. That conversation with dear old Dad about the agreements between Rowling Energy and the Montoros—the one he'd promised Gabriel he'd have—never had to happen.

Liverpool was the perfect solution to his relationship with Bella—if they had to lie low, what better place to do it than England?

But he couldn't get enthusiastic about it all at once. Bella deserved better than to be required to hide their relationship because of his past. She shouldn't have to move to England if she wanted to be with him, just because he couldn't get another contract.

How had things grown so complicated so fast? The king of uncomplicating things was falling down on the job.

"I need some time to weigh my options," James announced suddenly. Because he'd just realized he not only had options, he also had other people to consider outside of himself. "I appreciate the offer, and it's generous under the circumstances. Mr. Stewart will update you soon on my decision."

Liverpool wasn't the right club for him. Not yet, maybe not ever. Not until he'd proven to everyone—Bella, his father, hell, even himself—that he could stop running away from conflict and deal with the consequences of his actions. He needed to be in Alma to do that. Permanently.

Actually, this wasn't very complicated at all.

James loved football. He'd thought for so long that a professional league contract was his goal, only to find the game had completely changed on him. Bella had changed it. He wanted to be a better man for her. She was the best reason of all to find out whether he could finally stand up under extreme pressure and come out a winner.

James hurried to Heathrow, eager to get back home and tell Bella that her belief in him wasn't misplaced. That he could be the hero she saw him as. He wanted to commit to her, to have a future with her.

As he settled back in his seat and switched off his cell phone in accordance with the flight attendant's instructions, he glanced at his watch. And cursed as he realized what was happening—it looked as if Will was going to be the lucky recipient of Grandfather's watch after all.

When James got off the plane in Del Sol, he powered up his cell phone intending to call Bella immediately. *Surprise. I'm home early.*

But the first text message that popped up was from Will.

Chelsea is here. You better come talk to her. She's camped out in the lobby disrupting business.

What the hell? He swore, dove into his Lamborghini and then drove to Rowling Energy at double the speed limit. The harrowing hairpin turns should have put a smile on his face the way they normally did, but Will's text message had effectively killed any cheer he might have taken from the thrill.

If only he'd called Chelsea back yesterday, when he'd seen the missed calls on his phone, the ensuing fiasco could have been avoided. But Bella had been nervous about confronting her father and he really didn't want to talk to Chelsea in the first place. So he'd ignored her. What could they possibly have to say to each other?

Apparently that had irritated his ex-girlfriend enough for her to go to Rowling Energy and bother his brother. James had dated her for…what, four months? Not long enough for her to remember that James hated Rowling Energy so much that he rarely set foot in the place. It had taken something as important to him as Bella to get him through the door last week.

His phone beeped. Will had texted him again. Hope you're almost here. Your ex is a piece of work.

Still fuming, James screeched into a parking spot and stomped into the elevator. Why in the hell had she taken it upon herself to disrupt an entire company in order to speak to an ex-lover she'd had no contact with for almost two years? When a bloke didn't ring you back, it meant he wasn't into you.

But when he arrived in the reception area, some of the pieces fell into place. Chelsea, looking less glamorous and far more worn than he recalled, sat on the leather couch bouncing a baby.

A baby.

Obviously she'd been busy since they'd broken up and was clearly hard up for money. What, did she think James was going to fund her for old times' sake? How dare she bring a kid in here as a sympathy ploy? His ire increased exponentially. She *was* a piece of work.

"Chelsea." She glanced up. "Can we take this outside please?"

She nodded, hoisted the baby to her hip and followed him out of the building to a shaded courtyard around the side of the building where employees sometimes ate lunch. It was thankfully deserted.

"You have a lot of nerve barging into my father's company to extort money from me," he said by way of greeting to the woman he'd had only marginal affection for once upon a time.

"That's not why I'm here and besides, you didn't

call me back," she reminded him as she settled onto a bench with the baby. "How else was I supposed to find you?"

He bit back a curse. "You're barking up the wrong tree if you think I'm going to give you a dime out of the goodness of my heart because some plonker knocked you up and you're short on cash."

That would explain why she had a bargain basement fashion statement going on. When they'd dated, she spent thousands on clothes and jewelry, usually with his credit card.

"Not someone." Chelsea peered up at him, totally cool. In her element because she'd gotten his attention after all. "You. This is your daughter."

His vision blacked out for a moment as all the blood rushed from his head.

I have a baby daughter. None of those words belonged in the same sentence. Blindly, James felt for the bench so he could sink onto it before the cramp in his stomach knocked him to the grass.

"What are you talking about?" he demanded hoarsely over the street sounds floating through the privacy bushes. "I haven't even seen you in almost two years. That's a baby and they only take nine months to make."

Chelsea smirked and flipped her lanky brown hair behind her back. "She's almost a year old, Daddy. Do the math."

Daddy. His brain couldn't—*could not*—keep up, especially when she insisted on throwing inflammatory monikers onto the woodpile. And now she wanted him to do subtraction on top of it all?

"Why...wha— How...?" Deep breath. His tongue couldn't seem to formulate the right questions. "Paternity test? I want one."

Okay, now he was on top of this situation. Get to the bottom of this pack of lies and toss her out on her no-longer-attractive rear end.

She rolled her eyes. "Fine. I'll arrange one as soon as possible. But there's really no question."

The little girl picked that moment to turn her head, peering directly at James for the first time.

Aqua eyes the exact color of his beamed at him through fringed lashes. Not only the exact color of his, but both Will and their late mother shared the rare shade.

His world tilted and slid quickly off the rails. The paternity test would be superfluous, obviously.

He couldn't tear his gaze away from the baby. His baby. It was real. This was his child, and until five minutes ago he'd had no idea she existed. He'd missed his daughter's birth, along with a ton of other milestones, which he mourned all at once. Chelsea could never rectify that crime.

"Why now, Chelsea? You should have bloody well shown up long before today with this news."

"I thought she was Hugh's." Chelsea shrugged nonchalantly as if they were discussing a pair of pants she'd found in her closet after they'd broken up. "He's the guy I left you for. I must have miscalculated my conception date, but I didn't realize it until recently when her eyes changed color. And I knew I couldn't keep this from you."

There was so much wrong with all of that, he hardly knew where to start. "What happened when her eyes changed color, Chelsea? Did you see dollar signs that Hugh couldn't match?"

"No." She frowned, pulling her full lips into a pout. "I thought it was right that you know about Maisey."

Maisey. His daughter's name was Maisey. And he'd had no say in it. Not that it was a horrible name, but if Chelsea had told him when she got pregnant, he might have been able to participate in the selection process. He'd have liked to name his daughter after his mum. Yet another thing this woman had stolen from him.

"If you thought about me at all, I'm sure it had more to do with things like child support."

He had to get over it and figure this out. Chelsea was his daughter's mother. Period. Like it or not, they were going to have some type of relationship for the next eighteen years, at least. Maybe longer.

Before she could deny her selfishness again, he eyed her. "What did Hugh think about your little error in calculation? Bet he wasn't so thrilled."

Chelsea looked away quickly but not before he saw the flash of guilt in her expression.

"He left you," James concluded grimly. "And you're skint."

She sighed. "Hugh refused to keep taking care of a kid that wasn't his and he might have been slightly ticked to find out that I fudged the details a little about the last time you and I slept together. So yeah, I'm low on money."

God, did the string of dumb decisions this woman had made ever end? This was his daughter's life Chelsea was playing around with, but she seemed to be treating it all like a big game.

The baby made a noise that sounded like a cross between a sob and a sigh and she captivated his attention instantly.

"What was that? Is she okay?" he whispered.

"She's a baby," Chelsea snapped impatiently. "That's what they do. Make noise. And cry. And poop."

This conversation had passed surreal ten minutes ago.

"What do you want from me?" he demanded.

Well, hell. It hardly mattered what she wanted. If this little breathing bundle of hair and pink outfit was his daughter, there was a lot more to consider than what the woman who'd given birth to her hoped to achieve. He had rights. He had options. And he would exercise both.

"I want you to be her father," Chelsea said simply.

"Done. We need to discuss child support and custody arrangements."

Reality blasted him like a freight train whistle. What was his life going to look like from now on? Did he need to reconsider Liverpool so he could be close to Chelsea in England? How would Bella feel about spending weekends with his infant daughter from now on?

He scrubbed at his face. *Bella*. God, this was going to be exactly what her father had predicted—a disaster. She deserved so much more than to be saddled with a boyfriend who had a kid. And what kind of new problems might this cause for her? An illegitimate child surely wasn't going to make her father suddenly approve of James.

"Nothing to discuss." Chelsea shook her head. "I don't want either one. I want you to take her. Forever. I'm signing over all my rights to you."

"You…what?"

Arms crossed mutinously like the immature woman she was, Chelsea scowled. "I'm done being a mum. I hate it. This is your fault, so you take her."

She said it as if they were discussing a stray dog. And she was making his choice easy. He didn't want such a selfish mum raising his daughter anyway. Sickened that he could have ever been intimate with this woman, he nodded grimly. "Seems like the best idea all the way around, then."

Single dad. The voice in his head wouldn't stop

screaming that phrase, over and over, and the place in his heart that belonged to Bella ached at this new reality. Just as he'd accepted that he not only *could* do a long-term, roots-into-the-ground relationship, he wanted to. But not like this, with such a huge complication as a surprise baby.

The timing was horrific. Because he'd just realized why this was so difficult, why he couldn't take the Liverpool contract. Why he was so worried about dropping this news on Bella—he was in love with her.

Eleven

By evening, James hadn't called.

Bella tried not to think about it. He was busy with Liverpool. She got that. The one time she'd tried to call him, it went straight to voice mail. Maybe his cell phone had died and he'd forgotten his charger.

If not that, there was a simple explanation for his silence and when he got her message, he'd call. No one would willingly face down her father without having some skin in the game. James had said he'd call and he would. He cared about her. She knew he did.

After a long night of tossing and turning, she had to find something to do to keep busy and the farmhouse still needed work. It kept her mind off the disloyal thoughts that had crept in overnight— that the distance between here and England had given James some perspective and his feelings had cooled after all. Just as she'd feared.

Or he'd decided a princess with a scandal-averse family was too much work for a guy who liked to play the field.

Discovering a bird's nest in the tree close to the back steps finally pulled her attention from her morose thoughts. She missed her own birds— she'd moved the macaws James had given her to the Playa Del Onda house since she hadn't planned to continue traveling back and forth. These baby birds filled the silence with high-pitched cheeps and she smiled as she watched them from an upstairs window.

It was a much-needed sign. Regardless of what happened with James and the news regarding his contract with Liverpool, she should go forward with conservation work. Birds would always need her and she liked having a purpose.

When she returned to Playa Del Onda, a maid met her in the foyer and announced Bella had a visitor in the salon.

James. Her heart did a twisty dance move in her chest. Of course she'd blown his silence out of proportion and they'd laugh over her silliness. Maybe he'd come straight from the airport and somehow she'd missed his call. As she dashed into the salon, she palmed her phone, already checking for the errant message.

It wasn't James, though, and the man standing by the window almost rendered her speechless. But she found her manners somehow.

"Mr. Rowling," Bella greeted James's father cautiously. "How nice to see you."

They'd met formally once before and she'd greeted him at Will's party, but this was the first time they'd spoken without others in attendance. Did James know he was here? Had he already talked to his father? If Gabriel had spoken to Mr. Rowling, he would have mentioned it to her. She was flying completely blind and nothing good could possibly come of this surprise meeting.

James's father didn't offer his hand but instead bowed as if they'd stumbled into a formal setting without her realizing it. "Princess Isabella. Thank you for seeing me on short notice."

"Of course." Mindful of her father's warning to

watch her step when dealing with matters important to the crown, she inclined her head graciously. "What can I do for you?"

"May we take a seat?" Mr. Rowling indicated the overstuffed and incredibly uncomfortable couch.

Sure, why not add more formality on top of the already overbearing deference of the elder Rowling? She perched on the cushion and waited for Patrick Rowling to get to the point.

He cleared his throat. "I realize that you and Will have agreed to part ways and that you are seeing my other son. You've made a terrible mistake and I'm here to ensure you understand the full extent of it."

Geez, first her father and now Patrick Rowling? It was as if everyone thought she could be talked out of her feelings if they just tried hard enough. "Will would be a bigger mistake. We aren't interested in each other."

Mr. Rowling held up a conciliatory hand. "I'm not here to talk about Will. Granted, there is sound sense in a match between you and my son, but even I understand that the heart isn't always sensible."

Confused and suspicious, she eyed James's father. "Then why are you here?"

That had come out a little more bluntly than intended, but he didn't seem bothered by her lack of decorum.

Clearing his throat, he leaned forward as if about to impart a secret. "The mistake you're making, the one I'm here to help you avoid, is putting your faith in James. He is not a good choice for any woman, least of all you."

Her temper boiled over but she schooled her features and bit back the nasty phrase she'd been about to say. This man didn't know her and he had a lot of nerve assuming he had insight into what kind of man would be good for her.

But the worse crime was that he didn't know his own son either. That, she could correct.

"James is an amazing man. I'm shocked his own father doesn't recognize that, but since it's clear you don't, despite ample opportunity to come to know your son, I'll tell you. He has a good heart, a generous nature and most of all, he cares about me."

Her voice rang with sincerity. Because she believed what she was saying. He'd call soon and they'd talk about the future. Everything was going to work out.

Mr. Rowling frowned. "I do so hate to disagree. But my son is a notorious womanizer with little regard for anyone's feelings other than his own. Surely you're aware of his indiscretions." He swept her with a pitying once-over. "God help you if you're not."

Foreboding slid down her spine and raised the hair on the back of her neck.

"You mean the photographs in the tabloids?" She crossed her arms, wondering if it would actually protect her against this man's venom. "I'm aware of them."

James had been very upfront about his brush with scandal. Whatever his father thought he was going to accomplish by bringing up the pictures wasn't going to work.

"Oh, no, Princess Isabella." He shook his head with a *tsk*. "I'm talking about James's illegitimate daughter."

Bella's skin iced over. "His…what?" she whispered.

Mr. Rowling watched her closely through narrowed eyes, and she suspected he'd finally come to the meat of the reason he'd casually dropped by.

"James has an infant daughter he fathered with

his last girlfriend. Shall I assume from your reaction that he hasn't mentioned any of this to you?"

"No," she admitted quietly as her pulse skipped a whole lot of beats. "I wasn't aware."

And of course there was a reason James hadn't told her. There had to be. Her mind scrambled to come up with one. But without James here to explain, she was only left with huge question marks and no answers.

In all that time at the farmhouse together, he'd never once thought to mention a baby he'd fathered with the girlfriend he'd stopped seeing nearly two years ago? Had she completely misread what he'd confessed to her about his feelings? None of this made any sense. Why would he talk about the implications of moving to England but not tell her he had a daughter?

It was a lie. Mr. Rowling was trying to cause problems. That was the only explanation.

Mr. Rowling eyed her and she didn't miss the crafty glint in his gaze. Neither of his sons took after this schemer in any way and it was a testament to James that he'd ended up with such an upstanding character.

"It's true," he said, somehow correctly interpreting

the set of her jaw. "James will confirm it and then you might ask why he's kept it from you. It's a consideration for a woman when choosing whom she has a relationship with, don't you think?"

Yes, a huge consideration. That's what he'd meant by James not being a good choice for her. Because he wasn't trustworthy.

She shook her head against the rebellious thoughts. This was a campaign to poison her against James, plain and simple, but why, she couldn't fathom. "He has his reasons for not telling me. Whatever they are, I can forgive him."

Because that's what people in a relationship did. Not that she had any practice—she'd never had one, never dreamed she'd have one that tested her in quite this way. But James was worth figuring it out.

"You realize, of course, that his daughter is illegitimate." Mr. Rowling countered smoothly. "You're still in line for the throne should something happen to Gabriel. Alma doesn't cater to that sort of impropriety in its monarchy, and citizens have no patience for royal scandals. Frankly, neither do I."

It was a veiled threat, one she understood all too

well after the discussion with Gabriel and her father about business between the crown and Rowling Energy. And blast it, he wasn't overstating the
point about her position or potential to be queen
one day. A princess couldn't drag an illegitimate
child through the world's headlines.

Her head started to pound as her father's warning
played over and over on an endless loop in her mind.
Gabriel wouldn't be on her side with this one, not
after what happened with Rafe and Emily and their
unexpected pregnancy. Not after she'd already forced
her brother to renegotiate agreements with Rowling, which would be very difficult to wade through
indeed if Mr. Rowling's threat was to be believed.

If she continued to be with James, the entire future
of Gabriel's reign—and indeed perhaps her own—
might be in jeopardy.

"Let me ask you another question, Princess Isabella."

The way he said that made her spine crawl but
she didn't correct him. Only her friends called her
Bella and this man was not in that group. A shame
since she'd hoped he would become her father-in-
law someday. That dream had rapidly evaporated
under his onslaught.

She nodded, too miserable to figure out how to make her voice work.

"What if she's not the only illegitimate child out there?"

God, he was right. The reality of it unleashed a wave of nausea through her stomach. James had made no secret of his playboy past. Since she'd never sat around in virginal white gowns either, it hadn't troubled her. Until now.

She very much feared she might throw up.

"If you weren't aware of the baby, you also probably aren't aware that her mother is here in Playa Del Onda visiting James." Mr. Rowling leaned forward, apparently oblivious to the hot poker he'd just shoved through Bella's chest. "I know you'd like to think that you're special. James has a particular talent with women. But the fact of the matter is that he still has very deep feelings for the mother of his child. Their relationship is far from over."

"That's not true," Bella gasped out. It couldn't be. She wasn't that naïve. "Anyway, James is in England."

The pitying look Mr. Rowling gave her nearly stopped her heart. "He's been back in Alma since yesterday."

"I trust James implicitly," she shot back and cursed the wobble in her voice. She did. But he'd come home from England and *hadn't called* and his silence was deafening. "Why are you telling me all of this?"

Mr. Rowling pursed his lips. "I'm simply making sure you are aware of what you are getting yourself into by refusing to see the truth about James. I have your best interests at heart."

She doubted that very much. But it didn't negate the accusations he'd brought against James. Her throat burned as she dragged breath into her lungs.

No. This was propaganda, plain and simple. She shook her head again as if she could make it all go away with the denial. "I need to talk to James."

"Of course," he agreed far too quickly. "I've said my piece. But before I go, please note that Will is still open to honoring the original marriage agreement."

With that parting comment, Mr. Rowling followed the butler out of the salon, leaving Bella hollowed out. She crawled onto her bed to lie in a tight ball, but nothing could ease the sick waves still sloshing through her abdomen.

Lies. All of it was lies. James could—and

would—straighten all of this out and then they'd deal with the issue of his illegitimate child. Somehow.

Except he still didn't answer her call. Twice.

This silence…it was killing her. If he was done with her, she deserved to hear it from him, face-to-face. Not from his father.

She had to know, once and for all. If he wouldn't answer the phone, she'd go to his house.

The Montoro town car had long been on the list of instantly admitted vehicles at the Rowling Mansion gates, so the driver didn't have to announce Bella's presence. As Mr. Rowling had said, James's green Lamborghini sat parked in the circular drive of the Rowling mansion.

Bella climbed out of the car, her gaze fastened to the Lamborghini, her heart sinking like a stone. James was home. And hadn't called. Nor would he answer his phone. The truth of Mr. Rowling's revelations burned at the back of her eyes but she refused to let the tears fall.

James would explain.

A woman's laugh floated to her on the breeze and Bella automatically turned toward the gazebo down the slope from the main drive. It was partially obscured by foliage but James was easy to make out. Even if she couldn't plainly see the watch on James's arm, Will didn't live here, and neither would he be at his father's house in the middle of the work day when he had a company to run.

The dark haired woman sitting in the gazebo with James faced away from Bella, but she'd bet every last euro in the royal treasury it was his former girlfriend. It didn't mean anything. They were probably talking about the daughter they shared. Patrick Rowling wasn't going to ruin her relationship with James.

Bella had come for answers and now she'd get them.

Feeling like a voyeur but unable to stop herself, she moved closer to catch what they were saying but the murmurs were inaudible. And then James threaded his fingers through the woman's hair and pulled her into a scorching kiss.

And it was a *kiss*, nothing friendly about it.

The back of Bella's neck heated as she watched the man she loved kiss another woman.

James was kissing another woman.

Brazenly. Passionately. Openly. As if he didn't care one bit whether anyone saw him.

His watch glinted in the late afternoon sun as he pulled the dark-haired woman closer, and the flash blinded Bella. Or maybe her vision had blurred because of the tears.

How long had she been playing the fool in this scenario—and was she truly the last to find out? Was everyone giggling behind their hands at her naïvety? Mr. Rowling had certainly known. This was going on in his house and as many times as she'd accused him of not knowing his son...*she* was the one who didn't know James.

It all swirled through her chest, crushing down with so much weight she thought her heart would cease to beat under the pressure.

Whirling, she fled back to the car, only holding back the flood of anguish long enough to tell the driver to take her home.

But when she finally barricaded herself in her room, it didn't feel like home at all. The only place she'd ever experienced the good, honest emotions of what a home should feel like was at the farmhouse. But it had all been a complete lie.

Still blinded by tears, she packed as much as she

could into the bag she'd lived out of during those brief, precious days with James as they cleaned up the Montoro legacy. Alma could make do without her because she couldn't stay here.

Everything is moving too fast, he'd said. He'd meant *she* was, with her expectations and ill-timed confessions. The whole time, he'd had a woman and a baby on the side. Or was *Bella* the side dish in this scenario?

Horrified that she'd almost single-handedly brought down the monarchy with her own gullibility, she flung clothes into bags faster. New York. She'd go to New York where there were no bad memories. Her friends in Miami would only grill her about James because she'd stupidly kept them up to the minute as things unfolded with her new romance.

And her brother Rafe would see through her instantly. She couldn't stand to be around people who knew her well.

Within an hour, she'd convinced Gabriel to concoct some story explaining her absence and numbly settled into the car as it drove her to the private airstrip where the Montoro jet waited to take her to New York. It was the perfect place to forget her troubles among the casual acquaintances she planned to look up when she got there.

The shorter her time in Alma grew, the more hollowed out she felt.

When her phone beeped, she nearly hurled it out the window. *James*. Finally, he'd remembered that she existed. She didn't care what he had to say, couldn't even bear to see his name on the screen. But a perverse need to cut her losses, once and for all, had her opening up the text so she could respond with something scathing and final.

I'm home. Came by, but Gabriel said you left. When will you be back? We need to talk.

She just bet he'd come by—to tell her he was in love with his daughter's mother. Or worse, to lie to her some more.

Bella didn't think twice before typing in her reply.

Not coming back. Have a nice life with your family.

Now she could shake Alma's dust off her feet and start over somewhere James and his new family weren't. New York was perfect, a nonstop party, and she intended to live it up. After all, she'd narrowly escaped making a huge mistake and now she had no responsibilities to anyone other than herself. Exactly the way she liked it.

But Bella cried every minute of the flight over the Atlantic. Apparently, she'd lost the ability to lie to herself about losing the man she loved.

Twelve

The Manhattan skyline glowed brightly, cheering Bella slightly. Of course, since leaving Alma, the definition of cheer had become: *doesn't make me dissolve into a puddle of tears.*

She stared out over the city that never slept, wishing there was one person out there she could connect with, who understood her and saw past the surface. None of her friends had so much as realized anything was wrong. They'd been partying continuously since this time last night. It was a wonder they hadn't dropped from exhaustion yet.

"Hey, Bella!" someone called from behind her in the crowded penthouse. "Come try these Jell-O shots. They're fab."

Bella sighed and ignored whomever it was because the last thing she needed was alcohol. It just made her even more weepy. Besides, they'd go back to their inane conversations about clothes and shoes whether she joined them or not, as they'd been doing for hours. That was the problem with hooking up with casual acquaintances—they didn't have anything in common.

But neither did she want to call her friends in Miami. The problem was that she didn't really fit in with the wealthy, spoiled crowd she used to run around with in Miami either. Maybe she hadn't for a long time and that was why she'd felt so much like a hurricane back home—she'd never had enough of a reason to slow down and stop spinning.

In Alma, she'd found a reason. Or at least she'd thought she had. But apparently her judgment was suspect.

The party grew unbearably louder as someone turned up the extensive surround sound system that had come with the condo when Rafael had purchased it from a music executive. A Kanye West song beat through the speakers and Bella's friends danced in an alcohol-induced frenzy. All she wanted to do was lie on the wooden floor of a farmhouse eating grapes with a British football player who'd likely already forgotten she existed.

Barricading herself in her room—after kicking out an amorous couple who had no sense of boundaries—she flopped onto the bed and pulled the bag she'd carried from the farmhouse into her arms to hold it tight.

The bag was a poor substitute for the man it reminded her of. But it was all she had. When would she stop missing him so much? When would her heart catch a clue that James had not one, but two females in his life who interested him a whole lot more than Bella?

Something crumpled inside the bag. Puzzled, she glanced inside, sure she'd emptied the bag some time ago.

The letters.

She'd totally forgotten about finding the cache of old, handwritten letters under the floorboards of the farmhouse. She'd meant to give them to Tía Isabella and with everything that had happened… well, it was too late now. Maybe she could mail them to her aunt.

When she pulled the letters from the bag, the

memories of what had happened right after she'd found the letters flooded her and she almost couldn't keep her grip on the string-bound lot of paper.

James holding her, loving her, filling her to the brim. They'd made love on that gorgeous bed with the carved flowers not moments after discovering the hiding place under the boards.

She couldn't stand it and tossed the letters onto the bedside table, drawing her knees up to her chest, rocking in a tight ball as if that alone would ward off the crushing sense of loss.

The letters teetered and fell to the ground, splitting the ancient knotted string holding them together. Papers fluttered in a semicircle. She groaned and crawled to the floor to pick them up.

Indiscretion. Illegitimate. Love.

The words flashed across her vision as she gathered the pages. She held one of the letters up to read it from the beginning, instantly intrigued to learn more about a story that apparently closely mirrored her own, if those were the major themes.

She read and read, and flipped the letter over to read the back. Then, with dawning horror and apprehension, she read the rest. *No!* It couldn't be. She must have misread.

With shaking fingers, she fumbled for her phone and speed-dialed Gabriel before checking the time. Well, it didn't matter if it was the middle of the night in Alma. Gabriel needed to make sense of this.

"What?" he growled and she heard Serafia murmur in the background. "This better be good."

"Rafael Montoro II wasn't the child of the king," she blurted out. "Grandfather. Our father's father. He wasn't the king's son. The letters. The queen's lover died in the war. And this means he was illegitimate. They were in love, but—"

"Bella. Stop. Breathe. What are you talking about? What letters?" Gabriel asked calmly.

Yes. Breathing sounded like a good plan. Maybe none of this would pan out as a problem. Maybe she'd read too much into the letters. Maybe they were fake and could be fully debunked. She gulped sweet oxygen into her lungs but her brain was still on Perma-Spin.

"I found some old letters. At the farmhouse. They say that our grandfather, Rafael the Second, wasn't really the king's son by blood. Wait." She pulled her phone from her ear, took snapshots of the most incriminating letter and sent the pictures to Gabriel. "Okay, read the letter and tell me I misunderstood. But I couldn't have. It says they kept the queen's affair a secret because the war had just started and the country was in turmoil."

Gabriel went quiet as he waited for the message to come through and then she heard him talking to Serafia as he switched over to speakerphone to examine the photo.

"These letters are worth authenticating," he concluded. "I'm not sure what it means but if this is true, we'll have to sort out the succession. I might not be the next in line."

"Why do you sound so thrilled?" Bella asked suspiciously. That was not the reaction she'd been expecting. "This is kind of a big deal."

"Because now there's a possibility that after the wedding, I might be able to focus on getting my wife pregnant instead of worrying about how to hold my head so the crown doesn't fall off."

Serafia laughed and she and Gabriel apparently forgot about Bella because their conversation was clearly not meant for outsiders.

"Hey, you guys, what do we do now?" she called

loudly before things progressed much further. Geez, didn't they ever give the lovey-dovey stuff a rest? "We need to know if this is for real, preferably before the coronation. But who would be the legitimate heir if it's not you?"

God, what a mess. Thankfully, she wasn't in Alma, potentially about to be swept into a much larger scandal than any she'd ever created on her own.

"Juan Carlos," Serafia confirmed. "Of course. If Rafael's line is not legitimate, the throne would fall to his sister, Isabella. I don't think she'd hesitate to pass it to her grandson. It's perfect, don't you think? Juan Carlos has long been one of the biggest advocates of the restoration of the monarchy. He'll be a great king."

Gabriel muttered his agreement. "Bella, send me the letters overnight, but make copies of everything before you do. Can you send them tonight?"

"Sure." It wasn't as if she had anything else to do.

And that was how an Alman princess with a broken heart ended up at an all-night Kinkos on Fifth Avenue, while her so-called friends drank her vodka and ruined her furniture.

When she got home, she kicked them all out so she could be alone with her misery.

JFK Airport had it in for James. This was the ninth time he'd flown into the airport and the ninth time his luggage had been lost.

"You know what, forget it," he told the clerk he'd been working with for the past hour to locate his bags. "I'll call customer service later."

After two delays at Heathrow, all James wanted to do was crawl into a hole and sleep, but he'd spent close to thirty-six hours already trying to get to Bella. He wasn't flaking out now.

The car service ride to the address Gabriel had given him took another forty-five minutes and he almost got out and walked to Bella's building four times. He worried his lip with his teeth until he reached the building and then had to deal with the doorman, who of course wasn't expecting anyone named James Rowling.

"Please," he begged the doorman. "Buzz Ms. Montoro and tell her I'm here."

It was a desperate gamble, and she might very well say, *James who?* But he had to see her so he could fix things. He might be too late. His father might have ruined everything, but he had to take this shot to prove to Bella that she could trust him. That he'd absolutely planned to tell her about Maisey but everything had happened too fast.

"No need. Here I am."

Bella's voice washed over him and he spun around instantly. And there she was, wearing one of those little dresses that killed him every time, and he wanted to rush to her to sweep her up in his arms.

But he didn't. Because he didn't understand why she'd left Alma without at least letting him explain what was happening with Maisey or why his life had spiraled out of control so quickly that he'd managed to lose her or why just looking at her made everything seem better without her saying a word.

"Hi," he said, and then his throat closed.

He'd practiced what he'd say for a day and a half, only to buckle when it mattered most. Figured.

"Hi," she repeated, and glanced at the doorman, who was watching them avidly. "Thanks, Carl. It's okay."

She motioned James over to the side of the lobby,

presumably so she could talk to him with a measure of privacy. "What are you doing here?"

"I wanted to talk to you." *Obviously.*

Off kilter, he ran a hand over his rumpled hair. Now that he was here, flying to New York without even calling first seemed like a stupid plan.

But when his father had smugly told him that he'd taken the liberty of informing Bella about Maisey, James had kind of lost it. And he'd never really regained his senses, especially not after his father made it clear that Bella wasn't interested in a bloke with an illegitimate child. As though it was all sorted and James should just bow out.

That wasn't happening. Because if Bella was indeed no longer interested in him because of Maisey, he wanted to hear it from Bella.

"So talk." She crossed her arms and he got another clue that things between them had progressed so far past the point of reasonable, there might be no saving their relationship. He was on such unfamiliar, unsteady ground, it might as well be quicksand.

The damage was far more widespread than he'd hoped. "Why did you leave before I could explain about Maisey?"

"Maisey? Is that your girlfriend's name?" Her eyes widened and she huffed out a little noise of disgust. "Surely you didn't expect me to sit around and wait for you to give me the boot."

"Maisey is my daughter," he countered quietly. "Chelsea is her mother. I'm sorry I didn't get a chance to tell you about this myself. I'm very unhappy with my father for interfering."

"Well, that couldn't have happened if you'd just told me from the beginning." He could tell by her narrowed gaze that she'd already tried and convicted him. "Why couldn't you be honest with me?"

"I was going to tell you. But you left first." With no clue as to where she was going. Was that her way of saying a lover with a kid was *no bueno*? Sweat dripped between his shoulder blades as he scrambled for the right thing to say. "Why didn't you wait for me to call like we discussed?"

"Wait for you to—are you mad at *me*? You're the one who should be on your knees begging my forgiveness. And you know what else? I don't have to explain myself to you!"

She stormed to the elevator and he followed her,

only just squeezing through the doors before they closed.

Obviously *that* hadn't been the right thing to say. And she was far more furious than he'd have ever dreamed. Yeah, he'd messed up by giving his father an opportunity to get between them, but hadn't he just flown thousands of miles to fix it? Shouldn't he at least get two minutes to make his case?

Or was it too late and was he just wasting his time?

"Actually," he countered as anxiety seized his lungs. "An explanation would be smashing. Because I don't understand why you don't want to hear what I have to say. I thought we were a couple who dealt with things together."

And now he was shouting back at her. Good thing the elevator was empty.

He'd thought they were headed for something permanent. He had little experience with that sort of thing, but he didn't think jetting off to another continent without so much as a conversation about the potential complexities was how you did it.

He'd *wanted* to talk to her about Maisey. To share his fears and ask her opinion. To feel less alone with this huge life-altering role change that had been dropped on him. Even the simple logistics of flying to New York hadn't been so simple, not the way it used to be. It had required him to sweet-talk Catalina, one of the Rowling maids, into babysitting Maisey—totally not her job, but Cat was the only person James trusted implicitly since they'd grown up together. As soon as he got back, finding a nanny for his daughter was priority number one.

She wheeled on him, staring down her nose at him, which was an impressive feat since he was a head taller. "A couple? Really? Do you tell Chelsea the same thing? I saw you two together. You must have had a good laugh at my expense."

"You saw me and *Chelsea* together? When?"

"The day I left Alma. Don't shake your head at me. I *saw* you. You were very cozy in that gazebo."

Gazebo? He'd never set foot in any gazebo.

"That would be a little difficult when Chelsea and I were in my lawyer's office signing paperwork to give me sole custody of Maisey." They'd obtained the results of the fastest paternity test available and then James had spent a good deal more cash greasing the works so he could be rid of Chelsea as soon as possible. "And then she immediately left to go back to England."

He'd been relieved to have it done. The meeting with his lawyers had taken far longer than he'd expected but he had to deal with that for his daughter's sake before he could untangle himself to go talk to Bella. Unfortunately, those few hours had given his father the perfect window of opportunity to drive a wedge between James and Bella.

"She...what?" For the first time since he'd entered the elevator, Bella's furious expression wavered.

"Yeah. I came to tell you everything but you'd apparently just left. Gabriel gave me some lame explanation, so I texted you, remember?"

The elevator dinged and the doors opened but Bella didn't move, her expression shell-shocked. Gently, he guided her out of the elevator and she led him to the door of one of the apartments down the hall.

Once they were alone in the condo, James raised his brows in silent question.

"I remember your text message. Clearly," Bella allowed. "If Chelsea left, who were you kissing in the gazebo?"

"Kissing? You thought I was kissing someone?" His temper rose again. "Thanks for the lack of trust, Bella. That's why you took off? Because you thought I was two-timing you?"

Suddenly furious he'd spent almost two days in pursuit of a woman who thought so little of him, he clasped his aching head and tried to calm down.

"What was I supposed to think, James?" she whispered and even in his fit of temper he heard the hurt and pain behind it. "Your father told me you still had feelings for Chelsea. I thought he was lying, so I went to the Rowling mansion to talk to you. Only to see you kissing a dark-haired woman. I wouldn't have believed it except for your watch."

She glanced at his bare arm and her face froze as he held it up. "You mean the watch I gave to Will?"

"Oh, my God."

In a flash, she fell to the ground in a heap and he dashed to her, hauling her into his arms before he thought better of it.

"Are you okay?" he asked as he helped her stand, his heart hammering. "Did you faint?"

"No. My knees just gave out." She peered up, her gaze swimming with tears as she clutched his shoulders, not quite in his embrace but not quite distancing herself either. "It was Will. The whole time."

He nodded grimly. Such was the reality of having a brother who looked like you. People often mistook them for each other, but not with such devastating consequences. "Welcome to the world of twins."

Now he understood her animosity. No wonder he'd felt as if he was on the wrong side of a raging bull. His father's interference had caused even more damage than James had known.

And who the hell had *Will* been kissing in the gazebo?

"Why didn't you tell me you gave him your watch? You always wore it. I know how much it means to you and I just…well, I never would have thought you'd…" Her eyes shut for a beat. "I know, I left before you could tell me. I'm sorry. I shouldn't have jumped to conclusions."

"Yeah, on that note. Why did you?"

His temper hadn't fully fled but it had been so long since he'd been this close to her, he couldn't quite make himself let her go. So he sated himself on the scent of her and let that soothe his riled nerves.

"You said everything was moving too fast," she reminded him. "It's not that I didn't trust you. You've always been honest with me, but… Chelsea's your child's mother. You didn't call and your father said you were home from England. Your car was in the drive and he dropped the news about a baby and tells me you have feelings for your old girlfriend. Maybe you thought it was the right thing to try again with her."

That was so far off the mark…and yet he could see the logic from her perspective. It was maddening, impossible, ridiculous. "Not for me. I love *you*."

"You do?" The awe in her face nearly undid him. Until she whacked his shoulder with her fist. "Then why didn't you call me when you got back from England?"

"Blimey, Bella. I'd just had the news about the baby dropped on me, too."

She recoiled. "Wait. You mean you *just* found out you had a daughter?" Her eyelids flew shut for a moment. "I thought…"

"What, you mean you thought I knew from the very beginning?" He swore. Everything made so much more sense. Scowling, he guided her to the couch. "We need to get better at communication, obviously. Then my father wouldn't have been able to cause all of these problems."

She nodded, chagrin running rampant across her expression. "I'm sorry. I told you I wasn't any good at relationships."

"We're supposed to be figuring it out together. Remember?" Without taking his gaze from hers, he held out his hand. "I promised not to let go. I plan to stick to that."

She clasped his hand solemnly, no hesitation. "Are you really in love with me?"

"Completely." Tenderly, he smoothed a stray hair from her cheek. "I'm sorry, too, sweetheart. I was trying to get everything settled in my barmy life before I settled things with you. I jumbled it all up."

This was entirely his fault. If he'd told her every minute what she meant to him, she might have very well marched up to Will and demanded to know what he was doing. And realized it wasn't James. None of this would have happened.

He'd been missing this goal since day one, yet kept kicking the ball exactly the same way. No wonder she'd assumed he didn't want her anymore.

"So are things settled?" She searched his gaze and a line appeared between her eyes. "What did you mean about Chelsea signing over custody? What happened?"

And then reality—his new reality—crashed over him. They'd only dealt with the past. The future was still a big, scary unknown.

James shook his head. "She dumped the diaper bag in my lap and told me she was too young to be tied down with a baby she hadn't asked for. Being a mum is apparently too hard and it's interfering with her parties."

"Oh, James." Her quiet gasp of sympathy tugged at something in his chest.

"I'm quite gobsmacked." This was the conversation he'd intended to have when he went to her house in Playa Del Onda. Only to find that she'd taken off for New York. "I have a daughter I never knew existed and now she's mine. I'm a single father."

And he'd have to relinquish his title as the king of uncomplicating things. There was no way to spin the situation differently. No matter how much he loved Bella, she had to decide if he was worth all the extra stuff that came along with the deal.

Now the question was…would she?

* * *

James was a single father.

When she'd seen James across the lobby, she'd assumed he'd come to grovel and planned to send him packing. But then the extent of his father's lies and manipulation had come out, changing everything. The instant James had held up his bare wrist, she'd known. He wasn't the man his father made him out to be. The explanation she'd sought, the forgiveness she knew she could offer—it had all been right there, if only she'd stayed in Alma.

Part of the fault in all of this lay with her. She shouldn't have been so quick to judge, so quick to believe the worst in him. So quick to whirl off and leave broken pieces of her relationship with James in her wake.

And still James had said he loved her. Those sweet words…she'd wanted to fall into his arms and say them back a hundred times. If only it were that simple.

But it wasn't.

"That's…a lot to take in," Bella allowed with a small smile. Her mind reeled in a hundred directions and none of them created the type of cohesion she sought. "How old is she?"

"Around ten months. I wish I knew what that meant in terms of development. When will she start walking, for example? It's something I *should* know, as a father. But I don't." He shut his eyes for a beat. "I'm learning as I go."

Her heart dipped. This must be so hard. How did you learn to be a father with no warning? James would have to get there fast and probably felt ill-equipped and completely unready. "You'll be a great father."

He'd stepped up. Just as she would have expected. James always did the right thing.

"I'd like you to meet her. If you want to."

"I do," she said eagerly and then the full reality of what was happening hit her.

Dear God, was *she* ready to be the mate of a single father? She barely felt like an adult herself half the time. When she'd confronted her father to demand her right to see James, she'd taken huge steps to become the settled, responsible person she wanted to be.

But she wouldn't exactly call herself mother material, not yet. Maybe in the future she could be, after she'd spent time alone with James and they'd both figured out how to be in a relationship. But they didn't have the luxury of that time. She couldn't decide in a few months that it was too much responsibility and whirl away, leaving a broken family in her wake. Like her own mother had.

She loved James. After everything, that was still true.

But was love enough when their relationship had so many complications, so many things going against it? Adding a child into the mix—an illegitimate one at that, which would reflect poorly on the royal family—only made it worse.

And in the spirit of figuring it out together, they had to talk about it.

"Your daughter is a…" She'd almost said a *problem*. "A blessing. But I'm a princess in a country very unforgiving of indiscretions. I'm still in line for the throne. You realize there's a potential for our relationship to…go over very badly, right?"

The tabloids would have a field day, eviscerating the royal family in the press. She was supposed to be forging alliances and solidifying the new monarchy in the country of her heritage. Not constantly dodging scandals.

"Yeah." He sighed as she gripped his hand tighter. "I know. We don't make any sense together and you should toss me to the curb this minute. I'm a lot of trouble."

Her heart fluttered in panic at the thought. But that's what they were talking about. Either they'd make a go of it or they'd part ways.

"Seems like you warned me how much trouble you were once upon a time."

Continually. He'd told her he was bad news from the start. She hadn't believed him then and she still didn't. James Rowling had character that couldn't be faked. His father couldn't see it, but Bella did. He was every inch her hero and the rest of the world would see that, too. She'd *help* them see it. And that decided it.

She smiled as she cupped James's face. The face of her future. "Turns out I like my man with a side of trouble. We have a lot of obstacles to leap. We always have. But I think you're worth it, James Rowling. Jump with me."

"Are you sure?" he asked cautiously even as he pressed his jaw more firmly into her hand. "You don't worry about losing out on your fun lifestyle and how Maisey will tie you down?"

Once, that might have been her sole consideration. No longer.

"The party scene is empty and unfulfilling." As she said the words, they felt right. She'd been growing up all along, becoming a woman she could be proud of, one ready for new challenges. "Maybe someone who hadn't had a chance to sow her wild oats might feel differently. But I don't regret moving on to a new phase of life. Just don't let go of my hand, okay?"

"Never." He grinned back. "You're right, by the way. My grandfather's watch is very special to me. Will bet me that I would ask you to marry me before Gabriel's coronation and the watch was the prize. I fought like hell to keep it, but in the end, it was only fair to hand it over."

"But you haven't asked me to marry you." Because she'd run off and almost ruined everything.

"No, I haven't. Allow me to rectify that." He dropped to one knee and captured her hand. "Isabella Montoro, I love you. I don't deserve a minute of your time, let alone forever, but I'm so lost without you. I have sole custody of my daughter and it's selfish to ask you to be an instant mother. Despite all of that, I'm asking you to marry me anyway. Let me treat you like a princess the rest of your life."

Just when she'd thought he couldn't possibly get any more romantic, he said something like that. How could she say no? "Before I decide, I have a very important question to ask."

"Anything," he said solemnly.

"Do I have to move to England?"

His laugh warmed her. "No. I turned down Liverpool. My heart is in Alma. With you."

"Oh." And then her ability to speak completely fled as she internalized what she'd almost missed out on—an amazing man who'd quietly been making her his top priority all along. "Then yes," she whispered. "The answer is always yes."

He yanked on her hand, spilling her into his lap, and kissed her breathless, over and over until she finally pushed on his chest.

"I love you, too," she proclaimed. "Even though you made a stupid bet with your brother that lost you a watch and almost lost you a fiancée. What if I'd said no? Would you still ha—?"

He kissed her. It was a very effective way to end an argument and she hoped he planned to use it a whole lot in the future.

Epilogue

Bella still loved Miami. Thanks to the double Montoro wedding that had concluded a mere hour ago, she'd gotten an opportunity to come back, see her friends and spend some alone time with James. Which was much needed now that they were settling into life with a baby.

James's arm slipped around her waist as he handed her a glass of champagne. Still a little misty from the ceremony where her brothers had married their brides, she smiled at the man she loved.

Bella sighed a little over the romantic kiss her brother Rafe shared with his new wife, Emily, as they stole a few moments together in a secluded corner. Of course, they probably didn't intend for anyone to see them, but Bella had been keeping her eye on her new sister-in-law. She'd been a little unsteady due to her pregnancy.

Serafia Montoro, Bella's other new sister-in-law, toasted Gabriel and laughed at something her new husband said. They were going to be just as happy together as Rafe and Emily, no question.

The reception was in full swing. Five hundred of the world's most influential people packed the party. The governor of Florida chatted with Bella's father, Rafael III, near the bar and many other of Montoro Enterprises' key partners were in attendance.

"You ready to do this with me soon?" James murmured in her ear.

She shivered, as she always did when he touched her. Looked at her. Breathed in her general direction. Oh, she had it bad and it was delicious.

But who could blame her when she'd fallen in love with the only man in the world who got her? The only man who settled the hurricane in her heart. She'd returned to Alma to meet his daughter, who was the most precious thing in the world. And she looked just like her father, which was a plus in Bella's book. She'd instantly bonded with the little sweetheart.

Then James had helped Bella launch a fledgling organization dubbed the Alma Wildlife Conservation Society. A graphic with twin macaws served as the logo and no one had to know she'd secretly named them Will and James.

It was a healthy reminder that things weren't always what they seemed. As long as she always communicated with James, no one could tear them apart. It was their personal relationship credo and they practiced it often.

Bella smiled at James. "I'm afraid I'm out of siblings so our wedding ceremony will have to star only us. And Maisey."

James cocked his head. "You'd want her to participate? Babies and weddings don't necessarily mix."

"Of course," Bella insisted fiercely. "She's my daughter, too."

Maisey had surprised everyone by uttering her first word last week—*bird*. Her proud father couldn't stop smiling and Bella had decided then and there to have another baby as soon as possible. *After* she and James got married.

The Montoros didn't need any new scandals.

Not long after she'd returned to Alma, Gabriel had appointed a royal committee to authenticate the letters Bella had found at the farmhouse. After careful and thorough examination and corroborating evidence culled from the official archives, the letters proved valid.

The late Rafael Montoro II wasn't the legitimate royal heir, which meant no one in his line was either. His grandson, Gabriel, and granddaughter, Bella, weren't eligible for the throne. The legitimate line for the throne shifted to Isabella Salazar nee Montoro, Rafael's sister, who was unfortunately too ill to take on her new role. Therefore, her grandson, Juan Carlos II, long the only Montoro with the right heart to lead his country, became the sole legitimate heir.

Despite Bella's willingness to brave the tabloids with James, to weather the storm over the unfortunate circumstances of his daughter's birth, in the end, no one paid much attention to Bella and James as the world's focus shifted to Juan Carlos.

Bella wasn't the only Montoro to express relief. Gabriel looked forward to spending time with his new wife instead of balancing his personal life with his public reign. Their cousin would take the throne of Alma, leaving the three Montoro siblings to their happily-ever-afters.

* * * * *